I picture the beautiful faces of the small ones we've helped deliver from their bondage, the many more to come, and I must believe that their budding lives are as precious in God's eyes as the lives of our tiny unformed babies now held safely in His arms…

Marietta, Ohio
June 1858

SECRETS OF WAYFARERS INN

Family Secrets
River of Life
All That Remains

All That Remains

TRACEY BATEMAN

Guideposts

New York

CHAPTER ONE

November 1858

Rain fell in torrents, bringing waves crashing—over and over—to the bank of the Ohio River. Hidden behind a large oak on the Virginia side of the river, Prudence waited alone, praying for the package that was to arrive tonight.

Two packages, one bulging with precious cargo, the note had said. Two adults, one of them heavily pregnant. Prudence always felt the weight of her responsibility to keep the runaways safe even more when they had little ones, even if they were still tucked in their mothers' wombs.

Thunder shook the sky, matching the roiling of her stomach, and she thought of her own secret, hidden deep inside her body. Another life she alone was responsible to protect. She hadn't told Jason yet. She would wait a little while longer, until she was sure the Lord would allow them to keep this one.

If only Jason could remember why they had accepted God's call in the first place. Prudence knew his concern was born of love, and that was the reason she couldn't admonish him for a lack of faith on nights such as this, when the pain in

1

his leg held him at home while she carried out the task. He would have faced the pain to come with her, but if she found herself in a situation where she must run, he would only slow her down. The admission felt like a betrayal, but they both knew the unspoken truth.

Each time she received new instructions in the hollowed-out oak tree, Jason hovered as she waited for the cover of darkness. Prudence could always feel his prayers as the danger rose, peaked, and finally subsided. Yet they were never fully out of danger. He would pray every minute she was gone and would not relax until they were safely tucked beneath the quilt she'd stitched with her own hands. He would hold her—too tightly—until morning.

But first she had to focus her thoughts on the package that should have already arrived. Prudence tried not to surrender to the sin of worry, but she couldn't resist the frown pulling at her lips as she looked through the brush toward the dock where her small boat lifted and crashed down with the waves. The storm had begun only a few moments ago, after she had rowed from the Ohio bank and tied the small vessel securely to the dock. How on earth would she ever row safely back to the other side in this weather? *Oh, Lord,* she silently prayed, *calm the winds and waves, if it be Thy will.* If not, she had to believe God would keep them safe in the midst of the storm.

A branch snapped behind her and she froze, then whipped around.

"Friend of a friend?" a voice whispered from the shadows.

"Friend of a friend."

"My father would be absolutely furious if he knew you were a woman." The amused voice accompanied the man who stepped out from behind a tree, his coat collar high and his hat low to protect him from the persistent rain.

"Wh-what do you mean, sir?"

"I mean, ma'am," he said, his shadowy form large and fearsome, "that we've lost five of my father's slaves in the past three years. And unless I miss my guess, that circumstance appears to be largely your doing."

The sickening feeling that rolled inside of her had nothing to do with her pregnancy, but it threatened to release the contents of her stomach all the same. His voice, his words, the way he spoke. This man was not a slave. Prudence's hands shook, causing the lantern to sway as she took a step closer and raised the light to get a view of his face.

She gasped and shrank from him, taking a step backward as she looked up into the pale eyes of a white man. Fear tightened her gut, and she thought of her poor Jason waiting for her at home. She thought about the dear child deep inside of her. She swayed, blackness swirling about her. As she felt herself fading from consciousness, she thought about the precious human cargo she had expected to meet tonight and help on the journey to freedom. Where were they?

Almighty God, into Thine hands I commend us all.

Marietta, Ohio
August

Janice Eastman reached with leaden arms through the foggy veil of her dream world, searching for something solid to hold on to as she awoke. Anything that explained the buzzing noise invading her slumber.

She sat up slowly, and her surroundings began to make sense. Goodness, she'd fallen asleep in the wing chair again. That explained why her neck felt so stiff. With a sigh she glanced toward the sound that had drawn her from another dream about her late husband, Lawrence. In her dreams, he disapproved of her buying an inn with her two best friends. In life, she would have seriously considered his thoughts on the matter, and he very likely would've won the argument. But he'd flown away into heaven without her, so he could just keep his opinion to himself as far as she was concerned.

The buzzing started again, and this time she recognized it for what it was. Lifting her cell phone from the table next to the chair, she saw her daughter's name staring back at her. A slight smile touched her lips as she answered. "Hi, honey. I'm sorry it took so long to answer. I was dreaming about your father again. You'd think after a year—"

"Dreaming? Mother!"

Janice sighed. "Oh, I know I shouldn't sleep during the day. I dozed off for just a few minutes." *What time is it anyway?*

"Mother!" Stacy said again. "Where. Is. Larry?"

"Larry?" Janice popped to her feet. "Oh my word. Larry!" How on earth could she have gone and fallen asleep when she was supposed to be taking care of her five-year-old grandson?

"Maybe he's with Aunt LuAnn or Aunt Tess?"

"Don't worry, Stace," she said with more calm than she felt. "I'll find him pronto and call you right back."

"Wait—Mom! Don't hang up!"

But Janice pressed the button to end the call without acknowledging she'd even heard. The last thing she needed right now was her daughter's panic added to her own.

She hurried toward the kitchen. "Larry!" If there was one thing her grandson liked above all else, it was getting into Miss LuAnn's cookies when Nana wasn't watching closely enough. And this seemed to be an opportune moment for the sneaky little guy. Janice smiled, picturing the guilty look in his big brown eyes. A bit of clanging reached her ears as she pushed open the door and stepped inside ready to bust him with cookies in his hands.

"Good gravy, Janice." Tess Wallace, Janice's lifelong friend and one of three partners in their inn venture, whipped around from the stove, then caught herself on the counter as she stumbled. The cup of tea in her other hand clattered against the saucer but righted itself with barely a slosh. "You nearly scared me to death. Warn a girl next time."

Janice scanned the kitchen from one end to the other, ignoring the admonishment. She had no time for that. "Where's Larry?"

With a shrug, Tess limped her way to the wooden table, spilling a bit more tea into her saucer before she reached her chair. "I haven't seen him. I thought you were watching him."

Not very well!

"I fell asleep, and he ran off." She cast a quick glance at Tess's ankle and debated whether to ask for help. Tess could do pretty much anything most of the time, and Janice relied on her in situations such as this. What an absolutely terrible time for Tess to hurt herself!

Guilt stabbed Janice's conscience. And what a horrible thing for her to even think. The night before, Tess had stepped down hard in a hole left by the landscapers. By the time LuAnn and Janice had heard the cries and reached her, the sprained ankle had already begun to turn color and swell. She shouldn't even be getting her own tea, let alone traipse around after a five-year-old boy. But what else could Janice do? LuAnn was out. "Stacy's going to have a cow if I don't call her back soon."

The phone in Janice's hand buzzed and Stacy's name popped onto the screen as if summoned by the words. Janice pressed Decline, and had to force herself not to beg for Tess's help. She hated to admit it, even to herself, but she was no good in a crisis.

"He's probably off chasing a moth around the house. Or exploring. You know how he is." Tess waved aside Janice's fear as though it were nothing. The way her friends dismissed her sometimes really burned her up, but the three of them had been besties—as the kids these days liked to say—since their first year of college, when they were practically kids themselves, so no sense making waves now.

"I'm sure you're right." She gathered in her bottom lip, trying to decide where to start first in the mammoth house. They were in the midst of renovations. Opening the Wayfarers Inn as a bed-and-breakfast had seemed like a wonderful adventure when Tess suggested it a couple of months ago. Janice had championed the idea and once LuAnn, their history buff friend, had discovered the treasure trove of history between the walls, there was no stopping them. Living with Stacy had gotten more than a little tiresome, and moving in with Stuart, her thirty-six-year-old son, hadn't been an option. As the town coroner, he got calls at all hours, and a woman Janice's age needed her sleep—but not when she was supposed to be keeping an eye on her grandson!

The sound of chair legs scraping against the floor pulled Janice back to Tess. Her friend rose without even sipping her tea. "I'll help you look for Larry. He has to be around here somewhere. Where have you looked?"

Janice hesitated, then took a deep breath and shook her head. "Tess, sit down. You can't walk around. You'll make that ankle worse. Just stay here and let me know if he shows up looking for a cookie."

"Don't be ridiculous. Of course I'll help. Where have you looked so far?"

Janice opened her mouth to continue the argument, then gave in. There was no time to argue.

"This was my first and only real thought. You know how he likes to sneak sweets."

Tess's eyes took on that merry glint she got when she was amused or delighted. "He does at that." Janice sent her friend a grateful smile.

"Where did you last see him?"

"Oh, playing on that tablet thing of his. He was right there with me in the living room. Next thing, I was waking up and he was gone."

"Okay, stay calm. The last thing we need right now is for you to panic."

Janice frowned and pulled herself to full height—which wasn't much—and squared her shoulders. "I do not panic."

Tess slung her arm around Janice's shoulders. "Of course you don't."

Janice gave a huff. "Stop patronizing me. I have to find Larry before Stacy blows a gasket."

Tess frowned. "Are you okay?"

"I'm fine. Let's just find my grandson."

They searched the bottom floor first, from the kitchen to the café just outside the door. Janice cast a nervous glance to the door heading into the basement. Surely he wouldn't have gone down there. She glanced to the old elevator that had been boarded up until they discovered it a few weeks ago. It was the only part of the first floor that was not yet completely finished. Largely because they were trying to decide whether to fix and use the ancient thing, or if it should be taken out and turned into a closet on each floor.

"Don't you even worry about the elevator," Tess said, her intuition intact as always. "You know it's closed off tighter than a drum." They walked slowly past the bar and through the other café door into the sitting area. "Have you checked the living and reception areas really well?" she added.

"Not really. I sort of pan—Well, I thought he'd most likely be in the kitchen." She ignored the sudden smirk on Tess's face, and sucked in a full breath. "Larry Eastman! Are you in here?" she called, as she left Tess standing at the door of the room. She looked behind every piece of furniture Larry could possibly hide behind.

"Well, he's not on this floor." Tess turned and limped out of the room into the foyer and cast a worried glance toward the stairs.

"Wait here," Janice said. "You can't do steps."

"Of course I can. You go on ahead, and I'll be up there before you're finished searching the second-floor rooms."

There was no way Larry could have gotten into the rooms, but she grabbed the keys from the drawer in the bar just in case. By the time Tess reached the open space on the second floor, Janice was ready to head up to the third floor. This time, she insisted Tess sit herself down and wait. "As much as I appreciate the offer, Tess, you're slowing me down," she said firmly. "Stay here and rest that ankle."

She searched the danger zones first, which covered pretty much anywhere on the third and fourth floors. As a general rule, Tory "Thorn" Thornton, their contractor, had declared the top two floors off limits, even or maybe especially to the three owners, as the workers restored and renovated—trying to keep as much of the original wood, blown-glass windows, and bits of history as possible. It was a slow process and the workers had been a bit on edge lately, especially since there had been yet another problem with the wiring.

But Janice ignored the irritated looks. Only Robin, the one woman on the crew, showed her any sympathy. No one had seen hide nor hair of Larry, and he seemed nowhere to be found.

When she returned from the fourth floor to the third, Janice stared with exasperation right at Tess, who had not stayed put but had climbed the steps.

"Tess! You have to sit. That ankle's as big as a bowling ball."

Tess shook her head, splashing red curls around her face. "Absolutely not until we find him." She glanced at Janice's hand as the phone buzzed for the fifth time in fifteen minutes. "You better get that before she calls the cops."

With a sigh, Janice prepared herself for an earful and touched the screen. "Yes, Stacy. We are still looking."

"Mom! It's been over twenty minutes." The panic in Stacy's voice went straight to Janice's heart. And truthfully, she was about to dial 911 herself.

"We haven't looked in the basement yet," Tess said as she hopped the bottom step and landed with a grunt on the first floor.

"Tess is going to look in the basement, and I'm heading to the backyard. If we don't find him in a few minutes, we'll call the police. But you know he's probably chasing butterflies or exploring." Her words echoed Tess's statement from moments ago.

"Mom, you have to find him. I'm on my way!" The line between them went dead.

"I can't go into the basement." Tess swept a gaze to her swelling ankle. "The steps are a lot steeper and deeper than these and the railing isn't as sturdy."

"Well, then who's going to..."

"Janice, you know I would if I could. But you said yourself I can barely walk."

Janice gasped as she looked in horror at the truth in her friend's sad eyes. "You know I'd die down there by myself! I don't even like that spooky place when you and LuAnn are with me."

Tess took Janice firmly by the shoulders, giving no indication that she was even a tiny bit concerned with her fears of the dark, tight spaces, or spiders, and steered her toward the basement door. "You can do it. This is for Larry."

Gathering in a shuddering breath, Janice glanced back at her friend. Of course, Tess couldn't take those stairs. Still... "Do you think one of the workers might...? Robin seems nice."

"Goodness, Janice. They're on overtime as it is. They don't have time to form a search party...unless we can't find him..."

Vines of fear slithered up from Janice's insides and wound themselves around her heart. The all-too-familiar beginning of anxiety began to tighten her chest and spread toward her shoulders. She stopped short a few feet from the basement door, forcing Tess to do the same behind her. Pressing her hand to her chest, Janice shook her head.

"Don't," Tess said firmly in her teacher voice, as though Janice were one of her former students. "You don't have time for an anxiety attack. Panic later. What if Larry fell down the stairs? Are you just going to leave him there?" Tess snatched the flashlight from the accent table next to the basement door and handed it over. "Take this in case the lights go out. Besides, you might need to look in the tunnel, and it's dark as midnight in there."

The thought of her little grandson finding his way into that dark place, where a century and a half earlier escaped slaves had stealthily made their way to the river beneath the inn, only elevated her anxiety. And Tess could've been a little less bossy about it, but that didn't mean she wasn't right.

"Take a deep breath," Tess said, her hands getting decidedly heavier on Janice's shoulders. She reached around and switched on the light over the stairs. That helped some.

Reaching up, Janice patted her friend's hand. "Go rest that ankle before it gets any bigger. I'll be fine."

"I'll wait right here at the top of the steps so you don't feel like you're alone down there."

Janice nodded, drew a shaky breath, and stepped down onto the first step. Her head spun a little, and she wrapped a white-knuckled grip around the railing. *One foot after the other.*

Tess fell back to her typical attempt at encouragement. "Remember, there's nothing to fear but fear itself."

"That never helps," Janice said.

"God hasn't given you a spirit of fear," Tess called down as Janice reached the midway point.

"That helps." She'd meant it facetiously but then realized it actually did help. How many times had she quoted that same verse in Second Timothy to her children when they were afraid? Did she trust God or didn't she?

"Make me brave," she whispered to the heavens. "Larry!" she called out. "You down here, baby boy?"

As she reached the next-to-the-last step, Janice heard the distinct sound of scraping, then a clatter and the slamming of a door. An instant of fear shot through her, followed by a wave of relief. "I heard something," she called up to Tess.

"Oh, thank the Lord."

"Larry! Where are you?" She moved toward the sounds she'd heard, picking up her steps. She frowned as she noted chunks of what looked like mud trailing along the basement floor. Had Larry somehow gotten out through the front and come around to the back door and tracked in dirt? Making a note to check the lock on the door leading to the loading area, she continued toward the scraping noise she had heard.

"It's okay, sweetie. Come on out. Nana's not mad." Not too much anyway, and more at herself for falling asleep than at the wandering boy.

There were eight small rooms, four on each side of a narrow hallway, which they now knew were used to hide weary slaves while they waited for transport up the river toward Canada. She stopped short in front of one of the small bedrooms. The entrance to the tunnel was hidden under this room. Surely Larry hadn't found his way to the passageway. How would he have even known about it? Janice didn't remember him ever being around when they'd shown it off to friends and family. Knowing she was going to have to go into the room and possibly the tight, dark space, Janice steeled herself and took in a deep breath, then pushed the door open. "Larry?"

No answer.

She switched on the light and looked around while her eyes adjusted. She frowned. The beautiful mahogany antique rocking chair Tess had discovered at a flea market of all places, and which LuAnn had lovingly restored, was tipped on its side. Was that the clatter she'd heard? Strange. If the door slamming had been this door, then Larry must've been in here and gotten spooked when he heard her call. Thank goodness the chair appeared to be in one piece. "Lawrence John! You best show your little behind pronto or Nana's going to spank it."

She should have done it last time he ran off after a bluebird. He'd just wanted to see how far it could fly without landing, but for goodness' sake, he'd gone two miles before they'd found him. She knew he didn't mean to be bad, he just had the most vivid curiosity about anything in nature. If he made it to adulthood without absently walking off a cliff, he'd likely be one of the most brilliant minds of his generation. But first, she had to find him.

In trepidation, she noted that, not only had the rocking chair been upended, but the stool that had been built by the original owners of the inn to hide the tunnel was also on its side, revealing the gaping hole. Her legs shook as she walked to the stool next to the cot-sized bed installed in all of the rooms down here. This room would ultimately be off limits, except for guided tours, because of what lay beneath the floor.

Kneeling, she shined the flashlight down the hole. At first glance, it appeared as though an adult couldn't possibly fit, but she knew from earlier examinations that it widened after the entrance. Her heart sped up and the familiar numbness spread across her jaw from left to right the way it did when she was about to go into a full-blown panic attack. *Oh, mercy.*

"Jesus, help me." There was absolutely no time for this. True, she had just about every fear possible, particularly of dark, closed-in spaces, but she had to find the strength to take the plunge and go find her grandbaby before he got more lost or, worse, hurt. What would Lawrence do if he were here? Janice rolled her eyes at her own question. She knew what her husband would have done. Barged right in with the arm of the Lord as his strength and found his namesake safe and sound.

"Well, Lawrence Eastman, I'll just show you, mister."

Turning around, she got on her hands and knees and backed into the tunnel, never more aware of the extra twenty pounds she'd packed on since Lawrence died. When she was through the hole, she stood up and, turning around, gripped the flashlight as though it were her last line of defense against an evil so terrifying she was starting to fear that the tightness in her chest might actually be "the big one" instead of just panic. Taking slow steps, she pressed her empty hand against the brick wall to steady herself.

"Janice!" Tess's voice sounded too near for her to have stayed upstairs. "Are you okay down there? You can come back. I found Larry."

She found Larry? Then who had knocked over the chair and stool? In her haste to turn back around and get to the tunnel, Janice got her feet tangled up and down she went. She landed hard on her backside, the flashlight flying from her hand. Everything went black.

Her imagination had always been her greatest weakness in times such as this. Not that there had ever been a time as wretched as this, except maybe during a couple of tornado warnings when Lawrence insisted they hunker down in a closet till it passed. But at least then she'd had her children to be strong for and her husband's strength to lean on. Right now, she was too utterly petrified to reach into the darkness and feel around for the flashlight. She knew it hadn't gone far. But there was no telling what she would grab. A snake? A rat?

Merciful heavenly Father, help me. She had to get out of here before she had an absolute panic attack.

"Janice? What are you doing in there?"

"I was looking for Larry." Obviously.

"Well, like I said, I found him. He's right here with me."

Thank goodness Tess hadn't left him upstairs in the main part of the house. No telling if he'd still be there when they returned.

"Hang on," Janice called. "I dropped the flashlight. Be there in a jiff."

She breathed in a steadying breath and forced herself to crawl farther into the tunnel. The bulky flashlight couldn't have rolled far. She inched her palms along the cold stone floor, her knees and hips protesting being placed in such a precarious position.

Against her nature and, frankly, her better judgment, she slid her hand along the floor until she made contact with an object she assumed was the flashlight.

"Found it," she called, inching her fingers forward, trying to find the handle. But as she felt along the object, she realized in one, awful, terrifying moment that this was no flashlight. With an ear-splitting scream, she chucked the object into the blackness, shooting to her feet without one thought for her poor knees or hips. As she rubbed her hands furiously on her pant legs, she heard sounds coming from her mouth she'd never heard before.

There wasn't any doubt. She'd grabbed the arm of a human skeleton.

CHAPTER TWO

U tter terror washed through Janice as childhood nightmares crashed around in her mind with lightning speed.
Her scream echoed off the tunnel walls and fear tightened
around her like bony fingers, squeezing the breath from her.

"Janice!" She heard Tess's voice but had no power to move,
to speak, to do anything but huddle against the cold brick wall
as far away from the fearsome remains as the narrow tunnel
allowed.

"Nana!"

The sound of her grandson's voice pierced through the
blinding fear and struck Janice's heart.

"Janice Eastman, you're scaring Larry. Now, you answer me
this second."

"I-I'm okay."

"Good grief. What on earth happened? Did your flashlight
go out? I knew we should've replaced those batteries."

"No. I dropped it."

"Do you still have your phone?"

Janice could've kicked herself. Of course she had her
phone. She felt around her wide sweater pocket until she
touched the smartphone, then wrapped her hand around it
like her life depended on it.

She'd heard somewhere that a fear of the dark was really one's fear of being *alone* in the dark, and she had to admit there was some truth to that. Just knowing Tess and Larry were mere feet away helped settle her nerves a tiny bit. She switched on her phone's flashlight and that helped even more. "I turned on the flashlight." But she had found a bone! Maybe her overactive imagination had convinced her it was a human arm. Maybe some poor animal had been trapped down here. Oh, she didn't like that thought at all.

"Okay, good," Tess said. "Now, get back here before you hurt yourself."

In all fairness to Tess, Janice had to admit that the main goal of this mission had been to find Larry, but really, couldn't Tess give her even a pat on the back for having braved the basement and the tunnel in the first place? Determination bolstered her as she straightened. Even at only five feet three inches tall, she barely had room above her head to stand upright and walk. Her thoughts traveled back in time one hundred and fifty years, and she imagined runaway slaves in tattered clothing negotiating the tunnel as they fled to freedom.

Did the arm bone belong to one of them? Now that she'd had a little time to get over her terror, Janice's natural curiosity, combined with the knowledge that Tess wasn't far away, moved her tentatively toward the skeletal remains. The light from her phone caused a shaky glow as she tried to keep her hand steady. At her feet, what were most definitely human bones lay scattered from skull to limbs, minus one hand and lower arm. Well, they would have to stay where they were until the experts arrived to remove them all and determine identity, if possible. There wasn't even a teeny, tiny chance that she was going to pick them up.

"Janice?" Tess's voice was edged with annoyance of her own. "Are you just going to stay in there all day? If so, Larry and I are going to go back upstairs and get a snack."

"I'm coming." With a sigh, Janice turned, casting one last glance at what she felt for sure were the remains of someone from an era gone by.

As the light scanned the wall, she caught a glimpse of something she hadn't seen before. A note? Or some kind of paper, maybe? Had someone had the nerve to leave a napkin or some other trash down here? Incensed at the very thought, Janice pictured herself marching right over there, picking it up, and giving a good piece of her mind to whoever the perpetrator was. But that would require actually going toward the bones instead of getting away from them as far and fast as humanly possible.

"Tess!" she called. "You won't believe it. One of the workers left trash down here. We're going to have to talk to them about that."

"The workers haven't gone near this section of tunnel."

Janice gathered a slow breath and exhaled. "Well, someone has been here."

"LuAnn might've accidentally dropped something. Just get it and come on."

What and walk past the dead person?

She almost headed for the entrance and left it, and probably would have done so as recently as two hours ago, so as not to prolong her time in the tunnel. But she had gone into the basement alone for the first time, which she hadn't known she could ever do. With a deep breath for courage, she reminded herself that she'd even come into the dark tunnel. If she could do those things, she could certainly walk two feet. After all, this was her inn too, and she was just as responsible as LuAnn and Tess to keep it tidy.

Rising onto the tiptoes of her tan slip-ons, she maneuvered tentatively around the bones. She flashed the light onto the paper. Only…She frowned as she knelt and picked it up. Her breath caught in her throat. It wasn't garbage at all but an old photograph—like the ones seen in museums and history books. The image was faded and hard to make out, and the edges were torn. Janice's heart picked up with excitement. She, Janice Eastman, had actually discovered a treasure. Not outgoing Tess or adventurous LuAnn. Her. It was too much to even take in right at this second, and she had no time to study the photograph with Larry and Tess waiting.

"You coming, Nana?"

Without even considering whether or not she should, Janice slid the photo into her pocket and headed for the tunnel entrance. By the time Tess and Larry pulled her into the little basement room, she was considering keeping it to herself until they figured out whose remains were lying in that tunnel.

"What took you so long?" Tess asked, curiosity shaping her features.

Casting a cautious glance at her grandson, Janice shook her head. "Let me help you, Tess." She positioned herself under

Tess's arm. Good grief, what had possessed her friend to come down here with that ankle? She could've sent a worker down to let her know Larry was back safe and sound. "Well?" Tess whispered.

"Later."

The photo and the remains might not even be related, she reasoned as she supported Tess going up the basement steps.

She had no time to fill anyone in on what she'd found as Stacy's breathless voice filled the room. "Oh, thank goodness. Come here, baby." She grabbed Larry and held him close, staring at Janice over his shoulder.

Larry wiggled out of her tight grasp. "Mommy, you're squishing me!"

Stacy's expression softened for the boy, and she held him at arm's length. There was no denying Larry was her life. Maybe a little too much of her life, if Janice were allowed to venture an opinion about it—which she wasn't.

"Where were you?" Stacy asked him. "I almost lost my mind."

Larry blinked at her, his expression confused. "How can you almost lose your mind?"

Stacy shook her head. "Well, never mind about that—it's just a saying. But you have to stop running off. You could've gotten kidnapped or hurt or ... well, a lot of things I don't even want to think about." She glanced up at Janice. "Where was he?"

Like a deer caught in headlights, Janice mimicked Larry's blink of innocence. "I'm not ... "

"You would not believe your mother." Tess stepped forward, curling her finger around Janice's shoulder and pulling her protectively to her side. "She went into that cold, dank basement all by herself."

"She screamed super loud." Larry's face brightened as he related the incident.

"You went exploring while Larry was missing?"

Seriously? Was the girl completely clueless? "When have I gone exploring anywhere, ever?" To say she'd never been the adventurous sort was an understatement of the highest degree. Janice was pretty sure that if she and Tess and LuAnn hadn't all been best friends in college, she'd have ended up a happy homebody and never ventured out for much more than grocery shopping, church, and the obligatory ladies' meetings. But between the other two women in her life, she'd been dragged from craft shows to conferences, they'd hiked the Grand Canyon one year when they were much younger, and she'd swam in the ocean and even went parasailing once. Well, she stayed in the boat while the other two went, but it was almost the same thing.

"Isaiah Wimber, one of the workers, brought him home," Tess said, her tone firm as she spoke to Stacy. "Your mother was in the basement *looking* for your son, babe, not exploring."

At Tess's words, Stacy's eyes narrowed. Janice held her breath waiting to find out if her daughter would accept the word of her adored "aunt" Tess. "All right. I'm sorry for saying that, Mom." Stacy's silky eyebrows rose. "Isaiah brought him home?"

The way she said his name with a slight lilt piqued Janice's curiosity, and she nodded.

With a quick, cautious glance at her mother, Stacy cleared her throat. "Well, make sure you thank him for me."

"You could go thank him yourself," Janice said, then regretted her hasty words. If Stacy had any interest in Isaiah, one teeny inkling that her mother approved would certainly nip it in the bud. "I mean, he did find our boy."

"About that, Mom..." Stacy said. "Is the inn too much for you? Why are you falling asleep during the day? Maybe you're taking on too much."

Seemingly unaware of the tension mounting between the adults, Larry grinned at his mother. "I found a bunny's nest." He stepped back and clasped his hands behind his back. "But I promise I didn't touch them."

Janice doubted the truth of the boy's words but didn't ask the questions that might bust him. She had her own secret. Sliding her hand inside her pocket, she felt the edges of the photograph. She'd have to let her friends know. But for now, it felt good to have something that was hers. Something she had discovered on her own instead of always tagging along while someone else took the lead. A smile tugged her lips as she thought of the adventure of the last few minutes, without a thought to the heart-stopping terror that had accompanied it.

"Well, we better get going. Larry, honey, go get your backpack. Mom, please think about what I said."

Larry frowned and ran into Janice's arms. "You said I get to stay all day with Nana. We didn't even have lunch."

Relishing the feel of his warm little body in her arms, Janice grinned and shrugged at Stacy over his head.

"I know, bud. But that was earlier. I took off work, so I get to spend the rest of the day with you. We could go to Over the Moon and have pizza."

Amazing how fast he disengaged from Janice's arms and turned to his mother with a curl-bouncing nod. "Okay!"

The mention of their favorite pizza place made Janice's mouth water, and she couldn't honestly blame Larry for his defection. The best he'd get at the inn was a grilled cheese or peanut butter and jelly sandwich, unless he wanted Winnie's homemade cream of mushroom soup—which there was no way he'd touch.

"Let's get you off that foot, Tess." Janice shook her head as they headed into the living room. "I wish I could convince Stacy we're doing the right thing with the inn."

"Oh, don't worry about her." Tess spoke through a grunt and a wince as Janice helped her settle in the wing chair, carefully propping her swollen ankle on a pillow placed strategically on the ottoman in front of her. "She'll come around when she sees how successful we're going to be."

"I know." Janice sighed. "I'll go get an ice pack for that ankle. It looks just awful."

"Then you have to tell me what you found in the basement." Tess's voice followed Janice to the door. "I know you didn't stay down there alone so long enjoying the atmosphere."

In the kitchen, Janice prepared the ice pack, then leaned against the counter, breathing out a sigh of relief for a minute alone. She reached into her pocket and pulled out the photo. The cracked, faded image caught her heart. It was hard to make out features, but the image was definitely a young black woman, a scarf on her head. Snuggled in her lap was a little girl of no more than three or four years old. Janice pressed the photograph to her chest and closed her eyes as she imagined who this could possibly be.

"Ms. Eastman? You okay?"

Janice squeaked, startled, and her eyes flew open at the intrusion. Isaiah Wimber stood at the back door frowning at her. "Isaiah. You scared me half to death. Yes, I'm fine. Just taking a minute."

"You praying?" The thirty-something man was about as handsome as God made them. His dark hair curling up at the bottom of his cap could use a trim. But his smile made her forget all about that. He'd always been polite, and his smile could brighten a dark room.

She and Lawrence had watched him grow from an ornery little boy to a lanky, smart-aleck teenager, to a handsome, faithful young man who never missed a church service. Why on earth Stacy hadn't chosen him was beyond Janice.

"No, I'm not praying. Just thinking. How's the third floor coming along?"

He shrugged his muscled contractor shoulders. "I probably shouldn't mention this, but we have to wait for tomorrow to finish the walls because James didn't make it in today. Tory wasn't too happy getting that call."

Tess wouldn't be happy about it either. That explained why Thorn had been dodging Tess all day. He hadn't wanted to tell her that James wasn't going to finish the wiring for the top two floors today. Janice had always believed they were pushing it, trying to open by Labor Day in the first place. Truth be told— and what she'd never admit to Stacy—she'd been so close to backing out of the whole thing once or twice. She and Lawrence had always lived a modest life. She'd clipped coupons and made simple, tasty meals. She'd shopped for Stacy's and Stuart's clothing in discount stores rather than the mall like their friends. For family vacations, they'd gone camping for a week rather than visiting Disney World, and she'd never driven a car less than ten years old. Could she really justify investing their hard-earned savings and her husband's life insurance in a venture that had a better chance of failing than succeeding? Did she really have the right to spend her children's inheritance?

"Ma'am?"

Isaiah's voice drew her from her reverie, and she shoved aside the weighty thoughts for now. "Sorry, I'm just gathering wool, as Mama used to say." She smiled at the young man.

With a chuckle, Isaiah walked to the refrigerator and pressed his plastic cup into the water dispenser. "No problem. I was just saying, don't worry about us having to stop on the third floor for the day. We aren't going home. I'm heading to the second floor to work on the flower room."

He grinned wide, and Janice wondered for a second if he'd ever given Stacy a second thought. She had been single since before Larry was born. Her no-good fiancé had seduced her, convincing her it was okay to live together since they were getting married. Oh, what a sorrow that bit of rebellion had been to her father. An embarrassment that the pastor's daughter wasn't living up to the standards Lawrence had preached with fiery passion, week in and week out.

The day Stacy discovered she was pregnant, the scoundrel had taken off, leaving her bitter and a shell of the bubbly, energetic girl she once had been. Destroying her dreams of becoming a doctor like her brother, who was four years her senior. Instead of applying for an internship, she'd settled for becoming a medical assistant and worked paycheck to paycheck to provide for her son and pay back student loans while living in a small rental house that she and Janice had shared since Lawrence's death—when they'd booted her out of the parsonage to make room for the young, hip new pastor and his bride.

Janice watched as Isaiah downed the whole cup of water and filled it again. "Thank you for bringing my grandson back to us."

He waved away her thanks. "No need for that. He's a good kid. I caught him just before he grabbed one of those baby rabbits, though."

Janice smiled. That explained why he could honestly say he hadn't touched one of them.

"I explained to him that the mommy bunny might not take care of it if she smelled human on her baby." He shrugged. "Pretty sure I convinced him. He's a smart kid, isn't he?"

"I think so." And he could use a daddy who thinks so. *Keep your mouth shut, Janice.* "His mother asked me to thank you also."

His face brightened, which delighted Janice. "Stacy's here? I might just go and say hello before I get back to work."

"No, she took Larry home for the rest of the day." His expression revealed fleeting disappointment, and Janice added, "But I'm sure she'd want to tell you in person. Just give her a call. You have her number?"

"No, ma'am."

"Well, I usually don't do this, but considering you did save her son..." She reached up and grabbed the marker next to a magnetized pad fixed to the refrigerator and quickly scribbled Stacy's number before she let her better judgment creep in and ruin the whole thing. She ripped it off and handed the little slip of paper to him. "Just..."

He grinned and winked as he stuffed it into his front shirt pocket. "Don't tell her you gave me the number? Don't worry. I got your back."

Janice chuckled. "I appreciate it." She grabbed the ice pack for Tess. "I best get this on Tess's ankle before it swells up any bigger. Thanks again."

Before she could move away from the counter, Isaiah reached out his big arms and engulfed her in a hug that squeezed the breath from her, then held on a little longer than a polite, church kind of hug. She gave him an awkward pat on the back just before he released her. He looked down at her with earnest hazel eyes. "I'm really sorry about Pastor. We miss him a lot. Not that we don't like Pastor Ben too."

Affection flooded over her, and she patted his arm. "We all miss Lawrence. But thank you for saying so." She didn't acknowledge what he'd said about the new pastor—a source of irritation for Janice. Why young people refused to take advice from experienced adults, she had no idea. She thought about this while she walked back through the house to the living room. The young pastor had virtually ignored all of her suggestions as though her thirty-five years as a pastor's wife meant nothing. Ben had gotten rid of the old baby grand piano for which Lawrence had led the fund-raising during his first year shepherding the little flock. The dear instrument had been shuffled off to who knew where and replaced with an electric keyboard, to name just one change.

This was the last straw as far as Janice was concerned. She'd been far too busy with Larry and the inn to address the matter of so many changes in such a short time with the young pastor, but she certainly intended to bring it up first chance she got. Truth be told—and Lord, forgive her—she'd forsaken the assembly for a solid month. She still went to her ladies' Bible study on Saturday mornings and, according to Ruby Meyers, there were so many changes she likely wouldn't recognize the place. They'd even replaced the two-and-a-half-foot wide, two-hundred-pound, solid-oak pulpit that Lawrence had stood behind every week. According to Ruby and the other ladies, a puny-looking metal thing stood pathetically in its place. Just awful. All the dignity and grace had been buried with Lawrence. He must be turning over in his grave.

"There you are. I thought you might've gotten lost again." Tess snickered at her own joke as Janice walked back into the living room.

Janice scowled. "I didn't get lost the first time."

"Oh, I know. Don't be so sensitive."

Carefully placing the ice pack on her friend's ankle, Janice gave her a sideways glance. "I'm never sensitive." Not without a good reason, anyway—drums in church for instance. Mercy!

"Whatever you say." There was a glint in Tess's eyes that no one could possibly resist.

Janice smiled, instantly forgiving her dear friend for anything and everything, real or imagined that had annoyed her today.

Tess smiled back. "Now sit down and tell me what is in that tunnel. And I can tell it's more than a piece of trash."

"I think we should wait for LuAnn." They had started this venture as a team, and Janice knew how she felt when she was left out of major information or decisions—not that there had been any of real significance.

"Wait for me about what?"

Their friend and partner breezed into the room a little breathless.

"There you are," Janice said, patting the cushion next to her. "How was lunch with Brad?"

LuAnn dropped to the couch. "It was fine. The food was good as always. Although Brad had to cut our lunch a little short and meet up with clients."

Janice and Tess gave each other a knowing look. In their minds it had definitely been a date.

Noting the look, LuAnn tossed an accent pillow at Tess, who laughed and caught it easily. "So what did you need to wait to tell me? Please don't tell me the interior designer isn't showing up again."

Tess shook her head. "She's running a little late but should be here by two. That gives us exactly one hour for Janice to spill it."

Janice felt a little proud to be the center of attention. That rarely happened. "First of all, I need to inform both of you that James didn't show up today, so the electricity on the third and fourth floors is delayed again."

"Oh, bother," Tess said.

"What do you mean he didn't show up?" LuAnn's eyes were clouded but not with irritation. She furrowed her brow in confusion.

Janice relayed what Isaiah had told her.

"But that's not true. I took the river road home and saw James with my own two eyes."

"So, if he was at the river, he wasn't at work," Tess pointed out. Janice nodded in agreement.

"Were you wearing your sunglasses?" Janice asked. "You know you don't see as well when you wear the really dark ones."

Shaking her head, LuAnn shifted on the couch. "I saw James coming out of the tunnel. Which reminds me, I am not crazy about the workmen using it at all, but especially in broad daylight. I don't want kids finding out where the opening is and going in and out. Tess, I don't mean to sound bossy, but we should all discuss it if we are going to start handing over the key for the tunnel entrance to the workers."

Tess blinked at her and frowned. "Me? Why would I?"

"Well, obviously Janice didn't know he was even at work, so she couldn't have given him the key."

Janice sniffed. "That's because he wasn't *at* work. Isaiah said so, and he's never been the sort to fib. I've known him practically his whole life."

"Isaiah who?" LuAnn asked.

Tess chuckled. "The one who looks like something out of a dream."

"Oh, Stacy's Isaiah." LuAnn winked at Janice.

"From your lips..." Janice said. "Anyway, he told me James didn't come in and that's why he's working in the flower room on the second floor."

"Flower room?" Tess said.

"Lilies and Lace. You know the guys feel too girlie calling it that." Janice waved to ward off another rabbit trail. She frowned. "It must have been James I heard down there when I thought it was Larry exploring." She turned her gaze on LuAnn. "Did you ask him why he was in the basement instead of finishing up the wiring?"

"No. He didn't see me. I stopped and called him, but he must not have heard me either." Tilting her head, LuAnn frowned again. "What do you mean you heard noise down there?"

Janice opened her mouth, but Tess spoke up first. "Our girl ventured all alone into the basement tunnel."

If they hadn't been friends for such a long time, LuAnn's shocked expression might have been insulting. But who was Janice trying to kid? She had always been the scaredy-cat of the trio and everyone knew it. "Why on earth did you do that?"

Between Janice and Tess talking over each other, they relayed the events of the past hour or so.

"Wow, you two have been hopping," LuAnn said.

"Ugh," Tess said, adjusting the pillow under her foot. "Don't remind me."

"You need to go see Stuart." LuAnn turned to Janice. "Do you think he could make time for Tess today?"

"I'll have him look at it when he gets here."

"Oh, he's already coming?" LuAnn beamed. "That's convenient. Tess won't have to walk on that foot to get to his office."

Tess frowned. "You didn't mention Stuart was coming."

Janice nodded, enjoying the drama of stretching out her discovery. "We need his services as coroner." With the passing of Dr. Stone, the oldest doctor in the history of practicing medicine as far as Janice was concerned, Stuart had been elected to fill the position.

"What on earth?" LuAnn said. "Who died?"

Holding up a finger, Janice pulled out her phone and pressed number one on speed dial. As usual, her son let it go to voice mail. "Stu, it's Mom. I need you to come over to the inn as soon as possible. It seems I've found a set of human bones."

CHAPTER THREE

A second after Janice finished leaving a voice mail for Stuart, her two friends pounced, tossing out questions that made Janice's head spin. Within five more minutes, she'd filled them in and she and LuAnn were standing over the bones. "You're right," LuAnn announced. "These are most certainly human bones."

Janice tried not to allow herself to become annoyed. She cringed inwardly at the display of emotions she'd experienced lately where her best friends in the entire world were concerned. She took in a breath to keep a snarky remark from darkening the door of her lips. "They look old to me."

LuAnn nodded. "I think you're right. Thankfully, you have a son who can look these over for us. Maybe we can keep it quiet."

"Why would we?" As much as she hated to admit it, Janice had been secretly looking forward to being the one the TV news wanted to speak to for a change. Lawrence had always taken center stage whenever some reporter decided to do a story on this or that regarding Christ Fellowship. And last month, Tess had been splashed all over the internet and national news when a photo of her being carried out of the inn by an overeager firefighter had gone viral. In reality, that had been a completely unnecessary so-called rescue. LuAnn had won teacher of the year so many times over the last thirty-five years, it was ridiculous—although admittedly, she truly deserved it each time. Home Economics teachers weren't going to get many accolades.

Turning a slight frown on Janice, LuAnn shrugged. "Well, nothing says 'pay for a night at a lovely historical inn' like a set of creepy human remains in the basement." She heaved a deep, troubled sigh. "You know we can't afford another setback."

Guilt pricked Janice at her dreams of grandeur. Of course this needed to be kept quiet if possible. "You're right. I wasn't thinking."

"What's that?"

At LuAnn's question, Janice glanced up from the bones and shoved aside her regret. She followed the glow of her friend's flashlight and felt her face warm. "I grabbed that bone earlier when I was fishing around for my flashlight. I might have panicked a little and flung it. D-do you want to pick it up?"

"Not in this lifetime. Who wouldn't have panicked?" She gave a shudder that made Janice feel better. Vindicated, somehow. "There's something leaning against the wall." LuAnn moved her head forward and squinted in the faint lighting. "It wasn't there when I came down here a few days ago to show James the sorts of soft lights we want along the walls." She snapped her fingers. "I know! I bet that's what he was doing earlier when I saw him come out of the tunnel. He was probably trying to figure out how to install those lights."

"That doesn't explain why he told Tory he wouldn't be here today," Janice said, as LuAnn headed for the object.

"Oh, well. We'll ask him later."

Janice's phone buzzed. She glanced down at the text. "It's from Tess. She wants us to take photos of the bones."

"Poor Tess." LuAnn chuckled. "She'd love to be down here."

"That is true." Janice sighed. "And I'd rather not."

"There's nothing wrong with that, Janice."

Drawing herself up to her full height, Janice took a deep breath to try to keep the negativity at bay. "However, I'd like to remind you exactly which of us found these bones in the first place." Her voice held a measure of confidence that she hoped masked the disappointment and frustration she felt at her own fear. As a pastor's wife, she'd learned pretty early on that there was a way to unruffle feathers and had used a soft tone to appease more than one disgruntled parishioner at Christ Fellowship over her years there. She only hoped it would work on herself.

LuAnn turned to her. "You were incredibly brave this morning, coming down here alone. Now, is something wrong?"

"Oh, nothing."

LuAnn walked back to her carrying a long sticklike object that Janice couldn't quite make out without turning her flashlight on her friend and half blinding her. "If anyone has done anything to hurt your feelings, I'd like to know. You know I'd never do anything intentionally to cause a rift between us."

Well, for goodness' sake. Now she felt like a real and utter heel. "You haven't, Lu. It's just been a long day, and I have a bit of a headache." Which was true on both counts. "What is that?" She nodded to the object in LuAnn's hand.

LuAnn hesitated for a second, peering closely at Janice, then held the item up for inspection. "It's just an old shovel. It must have been left outside for a long time because it's covered in dried mud and rust."

"Maybe we should leave it down here for Stu to look at."

"I don't think a shovel is under his jurisdiction as a coroner, do you?"

"Well, if someone used it to dig up these bones, don't you think it falls to the authorities to take it into evidence?"

"You watch too much *CSI*."

"Well, you don't watch enough, obviously." Janice tried to sound lighthearted. "Now you'll have to be fingerprinted to rule your prints out."

"Out of what?"

"The list of suspects. You of all people should know what that is." LuAnn's organizational skills and obsession with list making had helped them solve two mysteries already, in just two months.

A tiny gasp shuddered through LuAnn. "Oh, Janice. You're absolutely right. What was I thinking?" She turned on her heel and put the shovel back where she'd found it against the stone wall. "Have you heard back from Stuart?"

"No. He likely won't even listen to his messages until he sees all of his scheduled patients today."

"Well, let's go back upstairs. Tess is texting me now."

"Let me snap a few photos for her first."

As Janice had predicted, Stuart arrived at precisely at 5:42. Except for cold and flu season, he only allowed patients to be scheduled until four thirty each day. That way he could get his paperwork done in time to leave the office by five thirty each weekday except for Tuesday, when he took the afternoon off to volunteer at a free clinic. As Janice led the way to the skeleton she'd found, her son turned to her with a look of disbelief. "Do you mean to tell me you came down here alone?"

"Yes, I did." For the life of her, Janice couldn't figure out why on earth some lucky young woman hadn't snatched up her son. But at age thirty-six, he didn't seem to be in any hurry to find a wife. As much as she adored little Larry, Janice had a lot more love to give to grandchildren. Maybe she should've had a couple more kids herself to have expanded the likelihood of multiple pitter-pattering toddlers running around her floors, but it was too late to dwell on that now.

"Mother, what's gotten into you? You could've fallen and broken your hip."

"I'm not old enough for you to worry about broken hips. And I had no choice. Tess has that ankle, and your nephew took off again. What was I supposed to do, wait for him to come back like a homing pigeon?"

He chuckled, reminding Janice so much of his father. "Yeah, Stacy was having a cow. Larry's little stunt made us shorthanded today."

"Your sister was pretty upset at me for his 'little stunt.'"

Keeping his attention on carefully placing the remains into the body bag he'd carried with him, Stu shrugged at her comment. "The kid runs off too much. Stacy needs to stop blaming everyone else and get him under control."

"He's curious about nature and goes off before he thinks of consequences." Even though it felt good to hear her son taking up for her and, she had to admit his words did soothe the guilt she felt, she couldn't allow anyone to criticize Larry. "He'll grow out of it."

"Hopefully." Stuart zipped up the body bag and grabbed the shovel with his gloved hands.

"Should you leave that for the police? I think it's evidence."

Stuart gathered in a breath and nodded. He seemed a little reluctant but put it back where he'd found it. Janice had the uneasy feeling he thought she might hurt herself on the old implement. "Don't worry. I won't be coming back down here anytime soon." Or ever again if she could help it.

"Probably for the best. I'll get these back to the morgue and look them over in better light. But Mom, I'm guessing these are not even from this century. They'll likely have to be sent to Ohio University in Athens. They're the closest university with a decent archaeology department."

"We can't keep our bones?"

He hung back to allow her to precede him up through the tunnel entrance. "Be careful. Hang on to the railing. And no, you can't keep the bones. Why would you want to?"

Disappointment slithered through Janice. She'd envisioned encasing them like she'd seen in museums and putting them on display with a plaque that said something like: THESE ARE THE BONES OF AN UNFORTUNATE RUNAWAY SLAVE. DISCOVERED BY JANICE EASTMAN, PROPRIETOR.

"Well, of course we don't want an old set of human remains. Don't be ridiculous. Do you think we ought to call the police just in case a crime has been committed?"

"I'll call them on the way to the morgue. They'll likely send a forensic team over to dust for prints and look for evidence. If these bones were a result of a homicide, it wasn't even close to recently, but it does look like someone dug up the bones and planted them there for you to find."

Too bad LuAnn hadn't heard him say that about dusting for prints. Too much *CSI*, indeed. "You'd best tell the others not to disturb the scene, either."

"Can't you just do it? I parked by the basement door. Unless you want me to carry a body bag out the front?" His voice hinted of humor, which didn't sit well. "That might not be good for business."

"Do whatever floats your boat," she returned. "I can certainly relay your message."

"You okay, Mom?"

Janice sighed. "I'm fine."

They reached the basement room, and Janice replaced the stool covering the tunnel entrance, then followed Stuart into the massive open space where construction had begun to renovate the basement area. Tess had instructed Thorn to concentrate their efforts on the first two floors so they could at least open up for soup and tea and start renting rooms on the second floor. Of course, they had to wait at least two more weeks until the renovation on the third and fourth floors were sufficiently completed so as not to pose a risk of injury should anyone venture up there against the posted signs. You just never could tell with people.

Stuart bent down and pressed a kiss to her cheek and all of her annoyance at him left in a flash. She smiled. "You be careful driving. And be sure to get something to eat."

His face softened into a tender smile that reminded her so much of his father she caught her breath.

"I'll call you later and let you know what I find out from these bones of yours. That was pretty brave of you to risk a dark, tight space to find Larry. It reminds me of the time you went after Sammy when he ran into that cave. Remember, that year we camped in Missouri?"

Janice smiled at the memory. Stuart had a stupid, fat cat he'd named Sammy. Stuart was only five at the time, and Stacy a few months old.

"I do remember, but I can't believe you do. You were so young." She chuckled. "You nearly panicked and your father was too big to fit in there, so it was either go in after him or listen to you whining until he came out on his own."

"You always came through when it mattered, Ma. Just like today." He smiled at her again. "Don't worry about Stacy. She'll realize she overreacted as soon as she needs a babysitter again. You know she feels a lot more peaceful knowing Larry's with you than letting him go to day care."

Janice wasn't so sure, but she returned her son's smile all the same. "That's what Tess says."

He reached for the basement door. "Speaking of Miss Tess, be sure to remind her to keep that ankle elevated and take ibuprofen every four hours to help with the inflammation. Ice packs every hour for twenty minutes, and she has to stay off of it except to use the restroom."

"She's not going to like that at all."

"Well, since she refuses to go get an X-ray, she has no choice, and if it doesn't get better in a couple of days, she'll have to have it looked at to make sure there's not a fracture." He shook his head. "I don't know why you ladies are so stubborn."

Janice chuckled again as he stepped outside toward the official coroner's van. "Because, at our age, we've earned the right to make our own decisions—even if they're folly to anyone else." She said the last bit pointedly. She was under no illusion about her son's opinion of her new business venture.

"If you say so." He shook his head. "I left an order at the pharmacy for a low-dose pain pill that she can fill if the ibuprofen isn't sufficient for her pain."

He hesitated and studied her for a second, the way he always did when there was something on his mind. Janice braced herself for bad news or a confession she'd rather not hear.

"Ma, this whole inn thing. Are you sure you want to do this? Your friends will understand. They're better set up for retirement than you are."

She reached up and patted his cheek as she had when he was just a boy. "You let your mother worry about her own finances."

He released a heavy breath and looked up, his eyes scanning the room. "It's just with Pop gone now, I think..." He shrugged and shook his head. "No, you're right. It's your decision and your life. Just know I'm here if you get in over your head."

Janice had to admit, the delays in construction, inspection issues, and now bones found in the basement had her nervous about her third of the inn. She was beginning to wonder if she was about to lose her shirt on this venture that, at the time, had seemed like a good idea. But she couldn't accept help from her children. It was her place to help them, not the other way around. Still, if things didn't start going their way soon, she might have no choice but to pull out of the partnership while she still had something left to lose.

November 1858

Prudence came to consciousness slowly, feeling her body swaying up and down on a hard, cramped surface. Rain sprayed across her face, and she turned her head in the darkness. She gasped as she realized her head was pressed against scratchy material and if she wasn't mistaken, on a full lap.

"Shh." A hand pressed against her shoulder. "You fainted," a soft female voice said.

"Where am I?"

"In the skiff. We couldn't wait."

The fuzzy cloud was beginning to lift from her brain. Her stomach clenched as fear gripped her. "There was a white man."

"At your service, ma'am." The male voice held an edge of tension as he navigated the waves. The rain had slowed significantly. The lightning had risen to the clouds, with only an occasional flash, but it was enough for her to observe the very large man rowing hard against the waves. "I apologize for frightening you. I should've introduced myself right off." His breath was labored with his efforts, and Prudence couldn't help but be grateful she had been spared the difficult task.

She sat up slowly, her head spinning and nausea churning her insides. She swallowed hard. "I don't understand."

Even shrouded in darkness, anyone could see he wasn't a runaway slave. What if this white man had been sent to catch them all?

What would happen to the package and her child? If the man in question was a spy, her identity would be revealed soon enough anyway. If he wasn't, the woman would be on her way to Canada within the next twenty-four hours and it wouldn't matter. There was always the risk of runaway slaves being caught after they left her care. And in that case, it was possible that they would be beaten or tortured, not only as punishment for trying to escape, but also to try to get them to reveal the identity of those who were trying to help. She'd never heard of a case where this had happened along her route, but she knew it happened in other places.

Prudence turned to the woman and did something she had never done before: introduced herself. "My name is Prudence," she whispered.

"Cecille, ma'am." The woman grimaced and adjusted her position in the bottom of the boat.

Alarm seized Prudence at the implication. "Has thy time come?"

Cecille shook her head. "Just uncomfortable. Ain't nowhere to sit that makes any difference though. I reckon I'm so big now, I'm just going to have to thank the Lord anyways."

"When we get where we are going, I'll rub thy back. That will help some." She remembered well the final days of carrying her own little Hope. Two beautiful breaths left her baby girl before she floated into the arms of Jesus. As long as this precious woman was in her care, she would do anything she could to alleviate her fears and soothe her discomfort. But she still needed to know more about the man currently rowing them the last few yards across the Ohio. Even in the darkness, she could see the dock coming close. She reached inside of her apron pocket and gasped.

"Looking for your pistol?" the man asked. "I found it when I carried you to the boat. Don't worry, I'll give it back after we get to shore and I can tell you our story and why I'm with Cecille. You have nothing to fear from me."

"I find that difficult to accept, considering the obvious."

"Yet you were the one carrying a gun."

Prudence would never use a weapon on one of God's children. She didn't believe in violence, but Jason insisted she take it with her.

A wave caught the boat and shoved it the last few feet into the bank. It landed with a jolt. Without giving Prudence an opportunity to comment, the man sprang into action. He hopped from the boat, the rope in his hand, and pulled it, along with the two women, farther up the embankment. "Where do we hide this?"

Prudence shook her head as she stood. "Just tie it up." He did so quickly. She reached down to assist Cecille, but the man touched her arm. "Let me," he said softly. He held out his hand to Prudence. "If you'll allow."

Secrets of Wayfarers Inn

Not wanting to succumb to rudeness without giving him the benefit of the doubt, Prudence grudgingly accepted his help and stepped out of the boat. "I thank thee."

"My pleasure," he responded, moving forward with long steps. He gently lifted Cecille to her feet and assisted her out of the boat. "Which way?"

Prudence hesitated. If she misjudged his intentions, she was putting not only herself and Jason at risk, but everyone connected with them. Not to mention her unborn child. But staying in the open wasn't an option either. Clearly, Cecille was a slave at a nearby plantation or home, and if anyone had discovered her absence, there could already be a search party heading their way. They had to move. Oh, how she wished Jason were here to help her make this decision. *Holy Father,* she silently prayed, *I humbly ask for Thy wisdom. Thy thoughts are higher than mine.*

"We have to get moving." His voice was gruff, a command.

Behind her, Cecille gave a slight gasp, just as the man's hand grabbed Prudence's arm in a bruising grip and jerked her toward the woods.

CHAPTER FOUR

So we'll have a slumber party right here at the inn," LuAnn announced amid protests from Tess. "That'll be fun, won't it, Janice?"

"That's just ridiculous. I won't have the two of you losing sleep because I stepped in a hole."

"Well, it was a deep one," Janice said. Poor Tess looked plumb miserable. Janice felt the guilt of her friend's pain all the way to her toes. She should never have let her help find Larry.

"Don't be stubborn, Tess," LuAnn admonished. "We'll be perfectly fine sleeping in here. You can have the couch, and I picked up a couple of small airbeds for Janice and me to use. We'll be comfortable enough."

Tess didn't have a chance to argue further, as Janice's phone rang. "It's Stuart."

"Just like I thought, Ma," he said when she answered. "The bones are pretty old."

"Well, we figured that. What are you going to do with them?"

"I put in a call to the university, and they're sending someone over to get them in the morning. I called Chief Mayfield. He doesn't want to bother you three tonight, so he's going to send a team over in the morning to inspect the tunnel. I promised him you wouldn't disturb the scene until they get there."

"Of course not." Tess certainly couldn't go down the steps, and the bravery inspired by the need to rescue Janice's grandson had faded. She wouldn't go down into that dark tunnel alone now even if someone offered to pay her.

"How's Miss Tess doing?"

"Stubborn. She wants to go home, but Lu and I think she should stay off the ankle."

"Well, she could likely make it home with you two helping her. But yes, she'll do better staying put with her foot up."

"Wait, I'm putting you on speakerphone," Janice said. "Say that last line again. Not the first part."

With a chuckle, he complied, and Tess's grimace indicated that she'd heard him loud and clear.

Janice said goodbye and disconnected the call. "You see? Even Stuart thinks you shouldn't bother trying to walk on the ankle tonight."

"All right. Fine. You win." Tess sighed. "What about the bones?"

"Oh, he said they're old. He's sending them to Ohio University in Athens to determine their actual age. The police are coming tomorrow to inspect the tunnel and do whatever it is needs to be done."

"Well," LuAnn said. "We know the bones weren't there a few days ago. So we need to figure out who put them there and why." Her voice held excitement, and Janice wanted to shake her. Was she forgetting about what she'd said earlier? That this might cause further delay in getting the inn up and running?

They heard a tap on the door and glanced up all at once. Robin, one of the workers who had helped Janice that afternoon, stood looking tentative as though not sure she should interrupt.

"Robin, honey," LuAnn said. "We thought all the workers had gone. Come in."

Robin smiled. "I hope you don't mind. I used your bathroom to wash up and change my clothes. I have to stop at the grocery store on the way home, and I hate the thought of anyone seeing me all dusty and dirty from work."

"Of course we don't mind. Gracious, I don't blame you." Janice smiled at the rosy-cheeked girl. Well, not *girl* she guessed. She was likely close to Stacy's age. But unlike Stacy, Robin smiled easily, showing deep dimples in both cheeks. Even her brown eyes, surrounded by long lashes, held a smile. Janice always loved looking at a smile that touched the eyes.

"Thank you, ladies. I heard you talking and wanted to check in on Miss Tess before I left."

Tess's expression softened. "That was so thoughtful. We were just discussing the fact that I am perfectly able to get to the car and take myself home. This is nothing more than a twisted ankle."

Tess was obviously trying to get someone on her side. But it was too late. She'd already agreed to stay the night and that was that.

Robin stepped into the room, carrying a backpack half-zipped and bursting with papers slung across one shoulder. "I don't know," she said, her brow furrowed as she bent and studied Tess's ankle, which looked almost as bad all wrapped up as it had before. "That looks awful. You're a lot braver than I would be." She glanced around at them all. "I'd be bawling like a baby."

"So would I." Janice grinned.

"Why don't you stay here and have dinner with us?" LuAnn invited. "Winnie has been trying out new soup recipes, and I know for a fact we have some of those wonderful cheese biscuits she made and froze yesterday."

Robin's eyes brightened and just when Janice thought she was about to accept, she shook her head. "Thank you, anyway, Miss Lu. I have to go. I have to, uh…"—she jerked her thumb toward the doorway—"get home right away and uh, feed my dog."

"Oh, you have a dog?" Janice said, smiling. "What kind is it?"

"Uh, well, it's uh…hard to say," stammered Robin. "Just a typical dog, but I think she's special."

"Well, that's okay," Tess said. "You run along and take care of your groceries and puppy."

Robin smiled with what Janice could only call relief. "If I can do anything for you ladies, please don't hesitate to ask." She nodded toward Tess's ankle. "I agree with these two. You should stay put and keep your foot elevated and iced."

"Well, that settles it," LuAnn announced as though Tess would simply accept the opinion of a non-physician as the final authority.

Robin laughed. "You ladies take care. I'll see you tomorrow."

They stayed quiet until they heard the bell on the front door ding twice—once when the door opened and once when it closed after the young woman.

"Do you think she really has a dog?" Tess asked.

Janice frowned and flopped onto the sofa. "What do you mean?"

"It just seemed to me she was trying to find an excuse not to stay to dinner."

"Oh, for goodness' sake," Janice said, thinking Tess's newly suspicious mind was seeing things that weren't there. Since they'd solved two mysteries in two months, she thought herself quite the Sherlock Holmes.

"Well," LuAnn said, "even if she was lying, who can blame a pretty young girl for not wanting to eat soup and biscuits with three old women?" She started to giggle. "She definitely hightailed it out of here, didn't she?"

Her amusement was catching, and Janice joined her laughter. "Poor thing."

"But why lie about having a dog just to get out of dinner?" Tess continued. "She had to go to the grocery store. She could've just said she needed to go so she didn't get home too late or something." She shrugged. "I can't understand someone who makes up a story when the truth would do just as well."

"Goodness, Tess," LuAnn said. "You don't even know she doesn't have a dog. You're just being a grump." She stood from the other end of the sofa and walked toward the door. "I'm going to warm up our dinner. I'm starving."

Tess put her hands on the arms of her chair like she was going to get up, but LuAnn stopped her. "Do not even think about it. Janice and I are your servants tonight, whether you like it or not. I'll bring you a tray when it's ready. In the meantime..." She walked to the coffee table and pulled a pill bottle from her purse. "I got these filled earlier. I know you're in a lot more pain than you're letting on."

Tess dismissed the pills with a roll of her eyes. "I'm not taking opioids. So you wasted your money."

LuAnn grinned. "No I didn't. I used your debit card."

Janice laughed at her friend's audacity. She would never have had the courage to do something like that. As a matter of fact, she'd been debating whether she should just go pick up the prescription herself. But of course she'd had every intention of paying for them out of her own funds. "Lu's right, Tess. Just take the pills. Stuart told me they're the mildest ones you can get. Just take one, and if you don't like the way it makes you feel we won't insist anymore. Please?"

Taking in a breath, Tess nodded and held out her hand. "Fine. But if I get addicted to these things, you'll have no one but yourselves to blame."

Handing her the bottle, LuAnn nodded. "Duly noted."

Within a few minutes, Tess was snoring lightly in the chair. Janice smiled and set aside the half-finished sweater she'd been knitting for Larry. She was making it a size too large knowing he was growing like a weed. Last year's sweaters wouldn't do for this year. She had let him pick the colors, and he chose blue and green. Not her first choice of a combination, but if that's what he wanted, that's what she was making for him.

LuAnn was just assembling Tess's tray when Janice wandered into the kitchen. "Don't bother. She's sound asleep."

"Finally. At least we won't have to hear her arguments for a while. I know for a fact she didn't sleep much last night, because I could hear her TV on half the night. I don't know why she keeps insisting it's just a little twist of the ankle when anyone can see how awful it is."

"She's never liked hospitals. You know that."

LuAnn filled two bowls with the soup and placed them on the table. She grabbed a pot holder. "You and I may as well eat in here, since Tess is sleeping," she said opening the oven. "It's too bad we can't sleep upstairs in our beds."

Since moving to town two months ago, LuAnn had been living with Tess. It only made sense for her to extend the arrangement until they could all move into the inn. They would occupy the fourth floor, which consisted of suites for each of them. But they'd decided to renovate their floor last so they could open the café as soon as possible. Janice just hoped there would be no more delays so they could carry on with at least that part of the plan.

LuAnn pulled the warm cheese biscuits from the oven and placed them in a bread basket.

Janice filled their water glasses and set their silverware on the table. As they sat down, her stomach growled so she kept the blessing short.

LuAnn reached for a biscuit. "So, what are we going to do about those bones?"

Janice glanced up from her bowl, spoon suspended halfway to her mouth. "What do you mean? I told you Stuart said someone is coming from Ohio University to pick them up and study them." She took the bite, then reached for her glass of water as an explosion of spice burned her tongue. Curious. Maybe they'd gotten the wrong soup from the refrigerator by mistake.

"Yes, yes." Crumbs dropped from the biscuit in LuAnn's hand as she waved it toward Janice. "I know that. What I mean is, what are we going to do about finding out who put them there?"

Janice thought about the photo still in her pocket. She wanted to share it with her friends. She really did. But something about the woman and child in the photo intrigued her.

LuAnn scraped her chair along the floor as she pushed back from the table and stood.

"What are you doing?" Janice asked. "You haven't finished your dinner." She'd barely begun.

"I need to get my notebook." She disappeared through the kitchen door and returned a minute later carrying her turquoise notebook with the silver lettering that spelled "Notes" on the front. She plopped down in her seat and as she scooted back up to the table, Janice saw that she was also carrying a letter or bill of some kind. "I found this on the floor by the coffee table," she said, handing the paper to Janice.

Janice took the paper and studied it. It was an electric bill, marked "past due."

"It's Robin's," said LuAnn, opening the notebook a few pages in and pulling the silver pen from the spiral binding. "It must have fallen out of her backpack."

"Well now I feel even more for her," said Janice.

"Let's get our suspect list made before we move on to that subject," said LuAnn.

"Don't you think it's a little soon to start writing down the names of suspects? I don't see how there could even be any yet. Plus, I suspect that..." She gave a little giggle. "Get it, suspect?"

Janice might have considered LuAnn's affectionate smile patronizing earlier, while she was in her mood. But now she took it for what it was and grinned in response.

"What do you suspect?" LuAnn said.

"Oh." Good grief. She'd been so amused with herself she'd almost forgotten what track her train of thought was chugging down. "I just wonder if maybe the bones were down there the whole time and we missed them before."

LuAnn shook her head. "I don't see how we could have. Brad has been down there too, and the building inspector. Then there's James, of course, because I saw him coming out of the tunnel earlier today." She gasped and started writing. "James has to be a suspect. Don't you think that's suspicious? Especially since no one gave him a key to the padlock."

Janice nodded. "Right, and we had it covered well enough that a person would've had to know the opening existed just to find it like that. And that was after he called in sick today." She grimaced. "I can't stand a person just taking off work willy-nilly."

"We don't know why he took off. And if he had something to do with the bones it certainly wasn't willy-nilly. It was for a reason."

"Why would a person plant an old set of bones in another person's tunnel?" Janice had completely forgotten her soup and rested her chin in the palm of her hand as she mused. "Do you think someone is trying to frame us for a murder?"

"From the eighteen hundreds? Janice, really."

Heat flooded Janice's face. What had she been thinking? Of course someone wasn't trying to frame them.

"I don't know why I said that." She laughed. "I think it's just been a long day and my brain is on overload." If she had a prayer of finding out who the woman in the photo was, she was going to have to start thinking more logically. Oh, who was she kidding? Maybe she should just hand it over to LuAnn. She was really the better detective.

LuAnn tapped her lower lip with the pen. "What motive could James have for planting the bones there?"

"And from where did he dig them up?" Janice shuddered. "That's just gross."

LuAnn took a bite of her lukewarm soup and wrinkled her nose. "You know, I'm not sure I care for this. Is mushroom soup supposed to have a kick?"

"I was wondering the same thing. My tongue is burning off after just a couple of bites."

They looked at each other and shouted, "Over the Moon pizza!"

Janice followed the sounds of voices onto the porch where she found LuAnn and Tess sitting at their small table with a pot of coffee and a plate with three giant cinnamon rolls. She glanced at her two friends, relieved that she wasn't the only one still wearing her robe and slippers but a little ashamed that the coffeepot was half empty—a sure sign they'd been up for awhile.

"There's our sleepyhead," Tess said, motioning Janice to a chair with an empty cup on the table in front of it. "We were just about to rouse you. The chief called. He's sending his forensics team around nine to scour the tunnel for clues. That gives us an hour."

Janice sat as LuAnn poured the steaming liquid into her cup. She gave her friend a grateful smile as she added cream and a spoonful of sugar.

"The two of you could have woken me up last night so I could at least change into my pajamas," Tess scolded. "What if the contractors had come in and caught me sleeping in my clothes?"

Janice noted with a little surprise that Tess must have roused in the night, because she was in her pajamas and a robe. Janice hadn't heard a thing. "We figured you needed the rest. You should've woken one of us to help you change."

Tess grinned. "I did."

LuAnn rolled her eyes. "She stepped on me when she got out of the recliner. By accident, so she says."

Janice laughed.

"We've been waiting for you," LuAnn said. Her notebook sat on the table in front of her, and she held the pen in one hand while she sipped her coffee with the other. "Take a cinnamon roll. I swear, Winnie never sleeps. She was here by six this morning."

"She doesn't want us going to McHappy's for donuts now that she's cooking for us," Tess said.

"You mean we can't go to McHappy's anymore? I love that place."

"Who doesn't?" Tess nodded. "We'll just have to keep it on the q.t."

Reaching for a cinnamon roll, Janice shook her head. "Goodness gracious goat. I must've slept like the dead. I didn't hear a thing."

Tess shrugged. "Winnie came in the back door. Now, speaking of the dead. Who do we think might have planted those bones, Lu?"

"My guess is James. He obviously had opportunity"—she looked at Tess over her reading glasses—"with me catching him coming out of the tunnel."

"If it really was him you saw." Tess bit into the enormous pastry. She closed her eyes and sighed. "Winnie is a godsend."

"It was him," LuAnn answered. "I saw him with my own two eyes. And boy, I agree with you about Winnie."

"Absolutely." Janice swallowed her bite and chased it with a sip of coffee. "So, James may have had opportunity, but what on earth motive could an electrician have for digging up a set of one-hundred-and-fifty-year-old bones?"

LuAnn gave her a sharp glance. Over her glasses, no less. She looked every bit the stern history teacher. "What makes you think they're that old?"

Janice lifted her shoulders. "I don't know for sure. I just have a feeling they might have belonged to a runaway slave or someone involved with the Underground Railroad."

Tess raised her eyebrows and nodded. "That's probably a reasonable guess. We already know they're not fresh."

Wrinkling her nose, Janice pushed back the rest of her breakfast. One thing her stomach couldn't take at mealtime was talk of dead bodies, and now she couldn't shake the image of the bones from her brain. Maybe LuAnn was right and she did watch too much *CSI*.

Clicking her pen, LuAnn glanced at her notebook. "So, back to James, then. Janice is right. What is his motive?"

The three of them sat in silence, clearly equally stumped. Finally, Tess spoke up. "We'll get back to him. What about Robin? She was acting pretty cagey yesterday."

"Robin?" Janice focused on Tess. "I can't believe that lovely young woman would be a grave robber and bones planter."

"Well, no one is talking about her looks."

Giving a vehement shake of her head, Janice dug in her heels. "I'm not talking about her looks either. Did LuAnn show you the bill she found?"

"She did," Tess said. "And I say that only adds to the likelihood of her being our perp. "There's all kinds of motives for people when they need money. And it did seem like she was covering herself for some reason."

Janice lifted her eyebrows. "Perp? Really? Robin owing money to the electric company doesn't make her a grave-robbing bones transplanter."

Tess leaned forward, reaching for her coffee cup. "That's not the point."

"Okay," LuAnn broke in, "let's give Tess a chance to present her evidence."

It was pretty plain to see LuAnn was more than ready to solve another case. But slandering a girl they didn't even know? Janice waved her hand. "Fine. But I refuse to believe that sweet girl would be involved in committing a felony."

Tess frowned. "Is grave robbing a felony or a misdemeanor?"

"I'll find out." LuAnn made a note. "But wouldn't it be less a crime and more archaeology? Considering the age of the bones?"

"That's a good point. If the perpetrator were in fact an archaeologist," Tess said with a pointed edge to her tone. "Which Robin isn't."

Sighing, Janice clamped her mouth shut. After all, they were going to give due diligence to all the suspects presented.

LuAnn rested the pen between her fingers and motioned for Tess to continue.

"Well, I didn't like the way she stayed at the inn after all the other workers were gone."

"She explained that," Janice said.

"She did, in fact." LuAnn nodded. "But we'll go ahead and make a note of it. Because if she were up to no good, she would've planned for all contingencies."

"And she knew very well I sprained this ankle the day before yesterday. So it would have been logical to assume we'd stay at the inn."

"Except we didn't stay here the night you actually sprained it," Janice reminded the others.

"That's a good point," LuAnn conceded. "Tess, what other reason do you have to suspect Robin? Aside from the fact that she used our restroom to clean up—which, I have to say, doesn't seem very incriminating to me. She was on her way to the grocery store, after all. I certainly wouldn't go out in public as dirty as the crew gets."

"Neither would I!" Janice said with a definitive nod.

"Be that as it may," Tess said. "The fact remains that she said she was going to the store, but when we asked her to stay for dinner, she suddenly had a dog."

"That's true," LuAnn said.

"Well, just because her story changed a little bit doesn't mean she left the bones," Janice said. "Maybe she had to stop at the store and pick up food for the dog."

LuAnn raised her eyebrows and tilted her head, looking at Tess. "She makes a good point."

Tess narrowed her eyes at them. "So we have a situation," she said. "You say Robin has a dog, and I say she doesn't. And she needs help with her electric bill. What would you two say to a little visit to Robin's apartment?"

LuAnn's face lit up. "I'd say you're a genius."

Janice looked at her best friends, knowing that, once again, she was being sucked into something that would, in the end, feel very much like parasailing. Except this time, she didn't think they'd let her stay in the boat.

CHAPTER FIVE

It didn't take the forensics team long to collect a few samples, dust for fingerprints on the walls, and leave with the rusty shovel that hadn't been disturbed since Janice and Stuart were in the tunnel the day before. The whole ordeal was rather anticlimactic and disappointing as far as Janice was concerned. Somehow, she had hoped for...more.

"Janice, pay attention. You're about to run me into a tree." Tess's voice broke into Janice's thoughts.

They'd stopped by Janice's house to retrieve the wheelchair Stacy had used when she'd broken her leg. The house was empty when they arrived, so apparently Stacy had taken Larry to day care after all. Just as well for today.

"Okay, there's Robin's apartment building," LuAnn said.

"You sure this is the place?" Janice asked as she parked Tess's wheelchair on the sidewalk in front of a three-story brick historic building that was likely two hundred years old. It had been renovated and made into apartments.

LuAnn stepped across the brick walk to the steps. "This is the address on the bill." She turned and looked at Tess. "There's no ramp. You'll have to wait here and be the lookout."

"Lookout?" Tess started to hoist herself from the wheelchair, but Janice clamped a hand to her shoulder to force her to stay put.

"Don't even think about it. We had a deal." They agreed to let Tess go with them as long as she didn't put undue pressure on her ankle, and she had relented. But that was a hard promise for Tess to keep.

With a sigh, she settled back down. "I suppose you're right. If you need to make a fast getaway, I'd just hold you back."

"Okay, do you have your phone handy?" Janice asked.

"Right here."

"Call if anyone shows up."

"Janice," LuAnn called, "let's go."

They located Robin's mailbox at the front entrance. "Do we really want to do this?" Janice asked as she realized the apartment they were looking for was on the third floor. "There's no elevator."

"Do you want to know the truth? Now, look. We've tackled a lot more than a few stairs together over the years. We can do this to ease Tess's mind about Robin. She'd do it for either one of us."

By the time they reached the third floor, neither LuAnn nor Janice had the capacity to speak. They leaned against the hallway wall until they caught their breath. "I'll never brag about being in great shape for my age again," LuAnn said after a couple of minutes. "I think we should buy a couple of treadmills for the inn."

"Or we could just join the Y," Janice suggested. "They give a hefty senior citizen discount."

They found the apartment all the way at the other end of the hall. Janice looked nervously behind them. "What if someone sees us?"

"Oh, nobody ever knows their neighbors anymore. Do you know yours?"

She had a point there, but that didn't mean Robin wasn't the exception.

"My nerves are shot," Janice whispered. "What if she keeps a big pit bull or Great Dane or something in there?"

"Janice, it's not going to come through the door and eat us." LuAnn laughed. "Just listen when I ring the doorbell."

Janice put her ear up to the door. LuAnn put her finger to the button next to the doorjamb and gave it a long push. Janice could hear the buzz coming from the apartment, but no matter how closely she listened, she didn't hear a dog whining or barking.

"It could be an old dog," she said. "Maybe it doesn't hear so well."

LuAnn knocked hard on the door a few times, but the result was the same. Silence.

LuAnn waved. "Well, let's get out of here. Tess is right. Robin lied about having a dog. Which is a disappointment, I have to say. I like her a lot."

"I'm disappointed about the dog too," Janice said as they started toward the stairs. "But I think it's a bit of a stretch to think Robin lying about having a dog has anything to do with the bones we found."

They stopped short as the door closest to the stairs opened, and a long-haired man in his twenties came out. He grinned. "Hi, ladies. You two lost?"

"No, we were uh, just looking for Robin," Janice said. "She doesn't appear to be home."

"Robin, huh? The chick at the end of the hall?" He nodded. "She asked me to keep an eye out for her mom and sister." He looked from one to the other and a suspicious look passed over his face, then he shrugged.

"Okay." LuAnn tugged Janice to the stairs. "Well, let her know we came by."

"Wait, she left a key for you." He turned back to his door. "I'll go get it. Hang on a sec. I'm not sure where I put it…"

They waited only long enough for him to disappear inside his apartment before they bolted down the steps, which were thankfully easier to descend than ascend. They flew as fast as two women in their midsixties could fly and shoved out the front door. Tess still held vigil on the sidewalk and turned as they bolted down the steps. Janice grabbed the wheelchair and they power walked to the car. "Get in there!" she said, between gasps of breath. "Lu, pop the trunk! Hurry."

Tess stood carefully. "What happened? Was the dog vicious?"

LuAnn unlocked the doors and slid into the driver's seat. Leaning over she opened the passenger door. "Get in, Tess. We'll tell you in a sec."

With adrenaline-fueled strength, Janice folded the wheelchair and hefted it into the trunk. She slammed it down and dove into the back seat, just as the scraggly-haired young man came out of the building, holding up what was presumably the spare key to Robin's apartment.

"Gun it!" Janice commanded.

They didn't slow down until a couple of blocks later when a red light forced them to stop.

"What on earth happened?" Tess asked. "You'd better tell me, pronto."

"Well," LuAnn said, "you were right about one thing. There was no hint of a dog in that apartment."

Now that her heart rate was returning to normal, Janice replayed the past few minutes in her mind. A bubble of laughter rose up in her and spilled over into a giggle. Tess turned with a frown on her face, but LuAnn's laughter from the front seat joined Janice's.

"Do you know what I wonder?" LuAnn said.

Janice nodded. "Which...one..." She could barely get words out around what had turned into deep, consuming laughter. "Which one of us did he think was Robin's sister?"

When they returned to the inn, Winnie was just cleaning up after a morning of cooking and freezing recipes.

"You ladies didn't eat much of my soup last night," she said disapprovingly. "You didn't like it?"

Janice and LuAnn exchanged glances as they sat down at the table. "Well, it was certainly the creamiest cream soup I've ever eaten," Janice said. Winnie gave a sharp nod as though Janice hadn't told her anything she didn't already know.

Janice turned to LuAnn. "Lu? What about you?" She knew she was passing the buck, but she would not be responsible for losing their bread and butter, literally and figuratively.

Once the café opened, it would be swarming, because Winnie would draw customers in, and they planned to use her name in their promotions. Luckily, she wasn't asking for a percentage above her salary. But it wouldn't surprise Janice if she did, and they'd likely give it to her too.

"Miss Lu?" Winnie said when the silence proved too long. "You got something to say to me?"

With a glare at Janice, LuAnn gathered in a deep breath like she did when she was thinking and about to speak at the same time. "The thing is, Winnie…"

"You didn't like my soup?" Her tone dared anyone to say anything, one single word against her food. Janice almost felt sorry for LuAnn, but she was too relieved it wasn't her on the sharp side of Winnie's discontent.

"Well, it was very spicy."

"Spicy?" Winnie frowned. "That ain't right."

"It almost burned my taste buds off," LuAnn said, clearly bolstered by Winnie's rare moment of uncertainty.

The cook marched to the refrigerator and pulled out the leftovers. She grabbed a spoon from the drawer, and without even warming the soup up, dipped her spoon and raised it to her lips. Then, without a word, she tossed the entire container—which thankfully was disposable—into the garbage. "That's the last time I cook without my glasses. I must've used red pepper instead of paprika."

Relief flooded over Janice and from the looks on LuAnn's and Tess's faces, they must be feeling the same way.

"I'll make it up to you ladies," Winnie said, yanking off her apron. "I'll just take myself to the market and pick up some more mushrooms and cream."

"Oh, Winnie," Janice said. "You don't have to do that. We already know what a wonderful cook you are. Those cinnamon rolls..." At the look of determination from Winnie, Janice let her words trail off.

"I promised you my special Hungarian mushroom soup, and I aim to deliver it. It'll be ready for your supper tonight or my mother will haunt me from beyond."

Janice shuddered. "Well, nobody wants any haunting from anywhere. We'll look forward to it. Thank you."

Winnie grabbed her purse and left through the back door.

Tess rested her chin on her palm, staring at the door. "I wonder if she should really be driving if she can't tell the difference between paprika and red pepper."

"Probably not," LuAnn said with a chuckle. "I'm not going to be the one to tell her that. But you know what I can't get out of my head?"

"Robin's non-dog?" Tess asked.

"Well, Robin, anyway." She bit her lip and stared at the stove for a few seconds before finally nodding and getting up from her seat at the table.

"What is it, Lu?" Tess asked, her own expression a little worried.

"If she'll lie about one thing, she'll lie about other things," LuAnn continued.

"Like bones," Janice chimed in, although she felt the same tug on her own strings of compassion as she thought about Robin not being able to pay her bills.

"Well, it doesn't mean she doesn't deserve a little kindness," LuAnn said. She gathered her purse and keys. "I have an errand to run."

"Wait for me." Janice rose from her seat.

"I'm not staying behind." Tess got up with a heavy hand of support on the table.

LuAnn slipped on her dark sunglasses, and Janice and Tess sent her inside the utility company office to pay Robin's bill. She'd only been living in Marietta for a couple of months, so they hoped no one would recognize her and spill the beans.

"I'd still like to know why she would dig up those bones and put them in the tunnel," Tess grumped, clearly in pain even though Janice and LuAnn insisted she use the wheelchair.

"You don't know that she did, Tess." Janice couldn't believe Robin had anything to do with it, even if she did lie a little. She herself had occasionally been known to stretch the truth to get out of awkward situations.

"Well, you don't know that she didn't."

"It makes more sense to me that James Avery did it."

"To what end? James has been an electrician in this town since he took over for his dad after graduation."

A knock on the driver's side car window startled them both, and they turned to see a grinning Brad Grimes looking through the window. Janice pushed the button so he could speak to them.

"Hi, Brad. What's up?" she said.

"Nothing much with me, but you ladies have those guilty looks on your faces. Where's your partner in crime?"

Janice cast a sidelong look at Tess, whose knowing expression spoke volumes. Brad and LuAnn were supposedly just friends, but anyone with eyes could see he was falling for their bachelorette friend. And Tess and Janice were convinced God had finally given LuAnn the love she'd been lacking her whole life. If only she could fully set aside her past hurts and trust that Brad was a good and godly man who wouldn't break her heart. "She's inside paying the electric bill. We didn't see any reason for us all to go in."

"Ah, okay." He turned and glanced at the door before looking from Janice to Tess with hope in his eyes. It was sweet, really, that he would stand there in the sweltering August heat just to wait for whatever time LuAnn would grant him today. "Have you had your lunch yet? I was just about to walk over to Bar-B-Cutie. Can I treat you ladies?"

"Sounds good to me," Tess enthused from the back seat. "If you don't mind being seen with a slightly broken woman."

With a frown, he poked his head farther inside and observed her leg resting on the seat. "You hurt yourself?" He shook his head. "Of course you did. That ankle looks pretty swollen."

"You should have seen it yesterday," Janice said. "It was twice that big. We're forcing her to stay off it."

"Good plan." He smiled. Janice could certainly see why someone would be attracted to Brad. His blue eyes were kind and his easy smile generous. He would be perfect for LuAnn.

"Brad?" At the sound of LuAnn's voice, he rose too quickly and knocked his head against the top of the window frame. Janice caught a glimpse of his pained expression as he stood upright to face LuAnn.

"Hi! I just noticed the car and thought I'd say hello."

"Oh, I'm glad you did. How was the showing yesterday?"

Janice had forgotten he got called away during their lunch the day before.

"Ask questions over lunch," Tess said, leaning forward toward the front seat. "Brad's taking us for barbecue."

Thirty minutes later, they were seated at a table covered in a red checkered cloth, their food in front of them, half eaten. The server had removed a chair to make room for Tess's wheelchair. Since Brad had been there for the mystery at the inn when they were trying to purchase it, and the mystery of the missing quilt last month, it only seemed right that he should be filled in on the bones as well.

"And you have no idea where they came from or who might have done it?" Brad asked.

That was another thing Janice liked about Brad: he always took them seriously. Their antics might amuse him, but when it mattered, he was always there and all in. As much as Janice had loved and admired Lawrence for his strength and his ability to love his flock of sometimes wayward sheep, he'd rarely taken her seriously. Well, maybe that wasn't fair. She had to admit that she'd loved making her husband laugh.

He had often felt the weight of his God-given responsibility and many times brought his stresses and struggles home with him. He'd told her more than once that knowing she and the children were there waiting for him was sometimes the only thing during the day that brought him joy. "Like Jesus enduring the cross for the joy set before Him," he'd said often throughout their three and a half decades together. And she was glad to be his place of comfort.

She felt a nudge to her ribs and glanced at Tess, who nodded toward the large front window. Following her gaze, Janice's eyes grew big. She couldn't believe it! James Avery stood by his truck, well as you please, talking to a man Janice had never seen before. She frowned. "Do you know who that is?" she asked Tess.

Their words had pulled LuAnn and Brad from their private conversation. LuAnn turned. "Who *who* is?"

"The man standing with James Avery."

LuAnn squinted, and Brad shook his head. "I've never seen him."

"Me neither," LuAnn said. "But I say we ought to have Thorn fire that man. He took another sick day today."

"And he's clearly healthy as a horse." Tess's voice rang with outrage. "Do we have anyone working for us who isn't a big liar?"

Janice covered her friend's hand with her own. "Isaiah isn't, as far as I know. And I'm pretty sure Thorn is trustworthy."

"Well," LuAnn said. "Let's go."

Brad blinked. "Go where?"

"Thank you so much for lunch, Brad." Giving him a kind smile, LuAnn slung her purse over her shoulder as Janice stood and took hold of Tess's chair. "We'll return the favor with dinner at the inn soon. But for now, we have to go."

Brad grinned and shook his head. "You ladies go on and do what you have to do." He chuckled as they left him sitting at the table with the bill.

As they piled out of the restaurant onto the sidewalk, Tess planted her uninjured foot on the concrete, forcing a stop. "What are we doing?"

LuAnn whipped around and stared hard at her. "We're going to follow James and find out exactly what on earth he's up to."

CHAPTER SIX

J anice screamed and squeezed her eyes shut tight as LuAnn
nearly sideswiped a delivery truck. Realizing they weren't
dead or maimed, she opened one eye and gasped, gripping the
dashboard as LuAnn whipped the car into the left lane and
gunned it through a yellow light.

"Good grief. Don't kill us all," Tess hollered from the back
seat.

Unbelievably, James hadn't seemed to notice the crazy
women following him so closely. It was a wonder they hadn't
been issued a citation. Something bounced up and down in
the back of the pickup as it swerved in and out of traffic. Janice
squinted, straining her neck forward. "What is that in the back
of his truck?"

"I don't know," LuAnn said, merging into the right lane
without using her turn signal. The car behind them blared its
horn, but she seemed oblivious. "It looks like a box."

Leaning forward, Tess peered between the seats. "A pine
box, if you ask me."

Janice looked incredulously at Tess, then turned her attention back to the road, wishing LuAnn was paying better attention. "You mean a casket?"

"I can't tell for sure," LuAnn said, leaning forward as she gripped the steering wheel, as though her white-knuckled grip would help her drive any safer.

"That's because you're wearing your dark sunglasses," Tess said. "I'm never letting you drive with those things on again."

"I don't know," Janice said. "It looks a little small to be a casket. Would one fit in the bed of a truck like that? It isn't hanging over the end."

"But the tailgate is down," Tess said. "What do you think is in there?"

Janice was beginning to think maybe LuAnn was onto something in suspecting James as their grave robber. "What if it's more bones?"

"So he really could be the grave robber," LuAnn said. The truck flew through an intersection just as the light turned from yellow to red. "Shoot!" LuAnn slammed on the brakes, screeching the tires. Tess jerked forward, then back.

LuAnn turned to her. "Put on your seat belt! What on earth do you think you're doing?"

Janice barely heard her two friends weigh the pros and cons of the seat belt law as she stared at the red light. "What motive could he possibly have?"

"What?" LuAnn asked, turning to her.

"James. What possible motive could a third-generation electrician have for planting a pile of old bones in our tunnel?" She shrugged. "I mean, he doesn't have an ancestor associated with the inn."

Tess clicked her seat belt. "That you know of."

"My point is," Janice pressed on, "that he wasn't one of those people trying to buy the inn to save the family name or whatever."

"So what is your point?" Tess asked. "The light's green, Lu."

"That he doesn't have a motive."

"Well, shoot again," LuAnn said. She pulled the car into the nearest grocery store parking lot and put it in Park. "We lost him."

"Do you think he saw us?" Janice asked.

"You mean the crazy women practically on his bumper for two miles through town?" Tess unbuckled her seat belt. "I'm sure he didn't."

"Oh, some people never notice something like that," LuAnn said. "Besides, even if he noticed us, he'd chalk it up to women drivers, or he might have been trying to ditch us since he called in sick when he clearly isn't."

"Should we interrogate him?" Janice asked. "Maybe he has a motive we just don't know anything about yet. He did sneak into the tunnel."

"Technically we only have proof that he snuck *out*," Tess said.

LuAnn sighed, slid the gearshift back into Drive, and inched the car forward to the road. "We might as well go back to the inn. Winnie washed all the new linen, so we can fix up the second-floor rooms with bedding and towels at least."

"Oh, let's!" Janice said. Every new step forward in their venture gave her hope it might actually work, until some crazy mishap or disgusting old bones made her rethink the whole thing. "You know what I think we should do? Try out the rooms tonight!"

"That sounds like fun," Tess said.

LuAnn glanced in the rearview mirror at Tess. "What about that ankle? Or do you think Janice should wheel you up the steps?" She grinned and returned her attention to driving.

"It's a lot better. I could make it up them with some help and the railing."

"Oh, I forgot about your ankle, Tess." Disappointment welled up in Janice. "Of course she can't make it upstairs."

"Oh no? I'll prove it to you the second we get back. It barely even hurts anymore."

LuAnn smirked in the rearview mirror. "Probably the pain pill you took with lunch."

Tess shrugged and conceded the point. "Well, I hate to be the one to keep us from the fun of staying in the guest rooms."

"You didn't even want to stay last night," Janice reminded her. "What's changed?"

"That was different. You two weren't giving me a choice."

"It's okay," Janice said, turning to smile at her friend. "We'll do it after your ankle is healed up."

"That's ridiculous."

LuAnn snickered. "We could always call the big strong fireman—what was his name?—O'Hara?—who saved you from the kitchen fire last month. He'd probably love to carry you upstairs.

"Just like Rhett Butler—oh, that's a bit of irony. O'Hara...Rhett Butler." Janice joined the laughter. "He might have a little crush."

Tess snorted. "On himself." But she grinned. "Okay, how 'bout this. We stop in and see Stu. If he says I can go upstairs, we'll stay in the new rooms."

Janice hesitated, a little too long apparently, because Tess quickly added, "No, of course we can't do that. It's not like we're popping by a friend's house for tea. He's probably too busy."

Feeling rotten, Janice shook her head. "No, I'm sure he'd be happy to take time to look at your ankle. You're his favorite after all."

Tess beamed, but LuAnn pouted. "What am I, chopped liver?"

"Oh, you two. You know full well he loves you both."

LuAnn pulled into the clinic, and the three of them went inside. LuAnn wheeled Tess to the waiting area while Janice approached the desk.

"Can I help you?" Stacy asked without even looking up from her computer.

"Yes."

She clicked a button, then gave Janice her attention. "Mom? What's wrong?" She stood. "Are you sick?"

Janice almost wished she were if that's what it would take to shake the wall Stacy had built up between them lately. "I'm fine, honey. It's Aunt Tess. She'd like Stu to take a look at her ankle."

A glance around the crowded waiting room brought a tense clench to Stacy's jaw, but her gaze rested on Tess and she nodded. "We'll fit her in pretty quick. He had a feeling you might show up anyway."

Janice smiled brightly and waved at Tess and Lu. *Please, Lord,* she inwardly prayed. *Show me how to fix whatever is wrong with Stacy and me. Forgive me if I've done anything to hurt her that I'm unaware of.*

"Mom?" Stu entered the reception area behind the desk and frowned, studying her face. "You're flushed. Everything okay?"

"With me." She smiled and accepted his hug across the counter. "If I'm flushed it's because Aunt Lu drives like a maniac. Aunt Tess would like you to take a look at her ankle if you have time. We'd like to stay at the inn tonight, and she thinks she can make it up the steps if we help her."

Rolling his eyes, he waved at them. "You three… Hang on. I'll go around and take a look in the waiting room."

Ten minutes later, he proclaimed her well enough to walk around with a walking boot, which his nurse had already brought into the waiting room. "Use this. The ankle is a lot better than it was yesterday, so it's doubtful there are any fractures."

Tess beamed at him. "See? I told you there was nothing to worry about."

"But, Aunt Tess, your blood pressure is a little high. I'm guessing part of the swelling yesterday was fluid. Watch your salt," he ordered in his stern doctor voice. "And about the ankle. Even though it's looking better, there was still an injury, and you need to stay off of it as much as possible. As your doctor, I do not recommend going up or down stairs, but as someone who grew up knowing you, I'm pretty sure you're going to anyway."

He turned to Janice. "Mom, once she gets upstairs, get an ice pack and one of the painkillers I prescribed."

"Stu," Stacy called from the desk, "Avi's on the phone. She said she tried to call your cell."

Janice jerked her gaze from her daughter's carefully disinterested expression to her son's face, which had suddenly gone red as a beet. He cleared his throat. "You're all done," he said to Tess. Bending, he kissed Janice on the cheek. "I'll talk to you later, Mom. He walked toward the desk. "Stace, tell Avi I'll call her back on my cell phone." He disappeared behind the door to the exam rooms.

Janice locked eyes with Stacy and raised her eyebrows as her daughter hung up the phone and cast a guilty glance her way. Janice marched right up to the desk, but Stacy held up her hands as though defending herself. "Don't ask me anything, Mom. I don't know a thing."

"Yes, you do. Is your brother seeing a girl?"

"A woman?" She rolled her eyes.

"At my age, anyone *your* age is a girl. Answer the question." She said it with a grin, hoping to soften her daughter enough for a little information.

But Stacy stood firm. "You'll have to ask him yourself." Her eyes twinkled. "I would certainly never tell you that"—leaning forward, she lowered her voice—"he's been driving to Athens after work twice a week for the last three months. And she's been here a few times. But you didn't hear any of that from me."

Janice grinned, suddenly caught up in a camaraderie with her daughter she hadn't experienced for a long time. "Have you met her?"

"I have but only because she came into the clinic. You know how Stu is, but three months..."

Unable to resist a laugh at her son's fear of commitment, Janice nodded. "That might be a record."

"So, do you want to watch an old movie and get Chinese tonight?" Stacy asked.

Immediately, Janice felt disappointment flood from her head to her toes. Of course she'd love to spend time with her daughter, but after all, it had been her idea for the slumber party. "We were going to sleep in the second-floor rooms. But I suppose..."

"Never mind," came Stacy's terse reply. "Just..."

"Sweetheart, they'll understand if I change our plans. Chinese and a movie sound lovely."

"Coming, Janice?"

Stacy rolled her eyes. "Never mind, Mother. You've got better things to do." She glanced over Janice's shoulder. "Looks like Aunt Tess is going to walk to the car. I'll have the nurse's aide bring the wheelchair out." She signaled to the aide just as the phone rang. She picked it up, turning her back on Janice.

Effectively dismissed, Janice met her friends at the door.

"Something wrong?" Tess asked.

"No. Let's just go."

LuAnn followed the aide out of the door he held open for them. "There's definitely something wrong," she said. "But we'll talk about it later."

Janice sat in silence, staring out the window as LuAnn drove them back to the inn. She tried to pray, but mostly her pleas to heaven seemed stopped by the dark clouds that had rolled in since they'd arrived at the clinic. The weather seemed somehow fitting. Would she ever find a way to mend whatever she'd apparently broken between herself and her daughter?

November 1858

Prudence tried to scream against the hand covering her mouth. She flailed her arms and legs without effect as terror rose in her breast. "Shut up," the man's gruff voice whispered against her ear. "You're going to get us killed."

"Please, Miss Prudence." Cecille's gentle whisper shook with fear, bringing Prudence to her senses.

"Look."

Prudence's gaze followed the man's pointing finger to the river, where she could just make out a dim light through the fog. Her heart rose to her throat. "Wh-who is it?"

"My guess," the man said, releasing her, "is it's the over-seer of our plantation and my older brother, Rafe. He runs things since our father's death." He grabbed a branch still holding on to a few stray leaves. "Stay here and keep your mouths shut."

"What does thee intend to do? Fight them with a branch?"

"No, I'm going to try to cover our tracks." He belly-crawled away from them. Everything inside of Prudence screamed for her to grab Cecille and run while they had the chance. "Why dost thou trust him?" she whispered.

"I got no choice, if I want to save my baby."

"I don't understand."

"My first child, a pretty little girl, looked white. The master stole her from me and give her to his wife. Doctor says she can't have no more babes or she'll join her own three baby girls in heaven." She gave a shuddering breath. "She took my baby and sent me to the fields. Logan decided to help me escape so I can keep this one."

Prudence filed away the man's name, and, before she could even reach out to comfort Cecille, he had returned, the entire front of him caked in mud and sand. "I covered our tracks as best I could," he said, his breathing labored. "Hopefully between the darkness and the fog, we'll have enough time and cover to get away." He tossed a wary glance to the river, where a boat was just coming up on the bank. "We have to go." He motioned for Prudence to lead the way, but Prudence hesitated. "Listen," he whispered. "Trust me, don't trust me. I don't care. But let me assure you, Rafe will not turn us over to the sheriff for a six-month sentence and a fine. He'll put a bullet in you and me and take Cecille back to the slave quarters until she gives birth. If the child is white like Felicity, he'll give it to his wife. If not, he'll sell it."

Prudence nodded and motioned for them to follow. Even after all the horrors she'd seen with her own two eyes, all the stories she'd been told by those she'd helped escape, it still broke her heart when children were ripped from their mothers' arms.

She led the way, moving cautiously through the brush and trees, only the layers of stockings and her husband's heavy coat sparing her legs and arms from cuts and scratches as they traveled a wide path toward the Riverfront House. Once they were safely in the tunnel, she'd have her answers.

"Are we getting close?" the man asked. "I'm not sure how much farther Cecille can walk."

Prudence halted and turned to study the young woman. He was right. She was bedraggled and exhausted. And even if her skirt was only half as heavy as Prudence's own from dragging the muddy earth, every step would still be like walking through quicksand while weighted down by rocks. "Our destination is not far."

He grabbed her arm, his enormous hand circling easily around the thickness of her coat. "What are you trying to pull, lady?"

"Unhand me, sir." Prudence gathered her courage and yanked away her arm. "As I have just told you, we shall arrive at safety soon. But," she said pointedly, "only if we continue to move."

"Do you think I am a fool?" He towered above her, his fearsome face twisted in anger and suspicion. "We've come this way three times. Who are you? Is this a trap?"

"I am who I claim to be."

"Then what? You suspect I am setting a trap for you?"

"Thee has said it, not I." She drew in a breath. "But that is not the reason I've been circling. It seemed only wise to do so, in case the men in the boat were following."

His breath clouded the air as he exhaled in frustration. "You are probably right. But the fact remains, ma'am, that Cecille must get to safety soon." He turned to Cecille. "Unless I miss my guess you are having pains?"

For the first time, Prudence noticed the grimace on Cecille's face. But the woman shook her head. "No, I'm fine."

"Thee is not fine. But thee is very brave, dear one." Prudence knew there was no choice but to lead them to the Riverfront House now. She couldn't risk Cecille delivering in the muddy woods.

They trudged forward, until the glow of the lanterns in the windows signaled that they were expected. Prudence stopped at the edge of the woods, her stomach sinking.

"We cannot go forward," she said. They watched from their hiding place as one of the men knocked hard on the large front door.

"Where else can we go?" the man asked, his tone still holding the gruff edge as though he blamed her for this turn of events.

Prudence searched her spinning brain for an answer. When the men didn't find what they were looking for, they would most certainly search the Stockport Mill next. That was the place Prudence had delivered the packages before the Riverfront House—much safer with the hidden rooms and tunnels—became available to them.

An unmistakable gasp of pain flew from Cecille's lips.

"Lady!" Logan cried. "Where else can we go? Please!"

Prudence knew of only one other place where Cecille would be safe.

Oh, dear Father, please give me Thy strength. Deliver me from my fears.

CHAPTER SEVEN

The inn was abuzz with excitement when they arrived. Tory Thornton met them at the door, his face spread with a rare smile.

"Is there good news, Thorn?" LuAnn asked, responding to his infectious grin.

"Please say yes," Tess said. "Or stop smiling like you have good news."

He chuckled. "Yes, ma'am. I'd say so. I wasn't all that keen to hire Robin, not knowing her at all, but boy am I glad I did."

Annoyance hit Janice. Why on earth wouldn't a hardworking, strong young woman be an asset to Thorn's team, even if she was a newcomer?

Janice listened to the muffled sound of power tools coming from the upper floors. "You mean Robin fixed the wiring problem?"

"Sure did. So we're back to work on the third and fourth floors."

"How did she do that?" Tess asked, her tone still clearly not warm and toasty toward Robin. "Are we going to be fined for using an electrician without a license?"

"No, ma'am. It turns out James was nothing but a liar. The wiring was all done. Just had to be hooked up to the circuit box."

"How did she know how to do that?"

He shrugged. "I don't ask questions. I just look at results."

"Well, we'll have to thank her. Is she up there?" Janice asked, pointing at the vaulted ceilings.

Thorn shook his head. "I let her go home early. Her neighbor called her and told her that her mother and sister had arrived." He shrugged and cleared his throat, clearly looking for an exit.

LuAnn hooked her hand through Tess's elbow. "We'll get out of your way and let you get back to work. Thanks for letting us know things are back on track."

He nodded and turned to go.

"Oh, and Thorn."

He turned back to them with a look of utter dread on his face. "Ma'am?"

"We're spending the night in the second-floor rooms, so if you get here in the morning before we're up and about, don't worry that we have squatters."

"Good to know, ma'am." He narrowed his gaze as it landed on Tess's ankle. He pursed his lips together as his eyebrows went up. "I'll let the crew know."

"Well," Tess said as they watched him wander back to the stairs. "Not much of a talker, is he?"

Janice chuckled. "Nope."

They settled into the kitchen a few minutes later. Winnie had returned from her outing to the grocery store and the room was bursting with the scents of onion, butter, and yeast. "That bread smells divine, Winnie."

Winnie nodded but didn't turn away from the pot she was stirring. Janice observed their cook as LuAnn poured them each a cup of coffee. Winnie was at least ten years younger than her employers, yet there was an air of authority and confidence surrounding her that always made Janice feel a little intimidated. She couldn't help but feel as though Winnie, though not educated in conventional terms, knew much more than she herself did about almost everything. And this was coming from someone who had taught home economics for thirty-five years to countless young people.

She knew she had warmed her nest well as a homemaker, cook, mother, and pastor's wife. But now that her children were grown, her husband with Jesus, what was she good for? When they'd discussed purchasing the inn, they'd discussed LuAnn running the kitchen, but Janice had assumed she would take some cooking responsibility. But with Winnie so competent and confident, Janice had slowly faded into the background and left major decisions in her and LuAnn's capable hands.

"How's the new soup coming along, Winnie?" LuAnn asked as she set the three cups on the table like an experienced server. Due, Janice guessed, to her years of working her way through college at a café.

Without turning, Winnie sent them a dismissive wave. "If you don't want the cream to curdle, you best not get me going. I have to watch it close."

Tess cast a knowing look at her friends. They really were deluding themselves that they were Winnie's bosses. She ran this kitchen and everyone knew it.

"So, that's good news about the wiring." Janice sipped her coffee, then wrinkled her nose and grabbed the sugar bowl from the center of the table.

"It's going to be harder to keep an eye on you-know-who now, though." Tess poured cream into her cup and stirred. "I wonder if she's the one who disconnected the wiring in the first place."

LuAnn included them both in an exaggerated wide-eyed look at Winnie and jerked her head toward the cook.

Winnie, clearly listening, glanced over her shoulder. "Y'all don't have to hide anything from me. I know all about the bones you found in the basement. I don't even want to think about how they got there. Most likely some poor fellow got stuck down there and starved to death."

Janice shuddered at the vivid image Winnie's words conjured.

"How'd you know about that, Winnie?"

"I have ears, don't I? You three don't exactly whisper." She set the pot on the cool burner behind it and turned, without giving them a chance to respond. She wiped her palms down the front of her apron and walked to the coffeepot, where she poured herself a cup, then joined them. "There. That's all done. You ladies want some soup for lunch?"

Shaking her head, LuAnn slid the cream and sugar toward her. "Brad treated us all to lunch at Bar-B-Cutie. But we're all staying in the inn tonight in the new rooms, so we'll have it for supper."

"Humph," Winnie said as she spooned two heaping teaspoons of sugar into her cup and picked up the cream jug.

"I don't see any sense paying good money for restaurant food when you have two good hands."

LuAnn's mouth tipped to one side, and Janice laughed outright.

"Well, we didn't pay for it." Clearly, Tess wasn't as amused by the scolding as Janice and LuAnn. "Besides, we were hungry."

Never one to back down, Winnie met Tess's challenging gaze head on. "You shouldn't be going anywhere on that foot. If you'd been here where you belong, I could've whipped you up one of those shrimp-and-crab salads you like. I have some fresh-made bread too. Wouldn't have taken thirty minutes to give you something you know you'd have liked better. And you wouldn't be hurting so bad right now. Plus, that bottled barbecue sauce probably gave you the heartburn."

"And it was well worth it," Tess said, emphatically.

LuAnn glanced at Janice and her smirk turned into a full-on smile, and the two of them started to laugh.

Tess gave them a sheepish grin and relented. "Okay, fine. I would have preferred the shrimp-and-crab salad. But the barbeque was very good as well."

Winnie sniffed. "If you say so." Her eyes scanned the three of them and she sighed, taking a sip of her coffee. "I don't know what you ladies have been up to today besides lunch, but if you ask me, you need to keep your nose out of this bone business."

"What do you mean?" Janice gave Winnie her most innocent look.

Grabbing up her cup, Winnie rolled her eyes and walked to the sink. "Don't tell me if you don't want to, but you should

know I see a lot more that goes on around here than you think."
Now, leave your cups in the sink, and I'll take care of them
when I come back up from the laundry room."

The friends exchanged looks. Letting the comment about
the bones slide for now, Janice frowned at their cook as she
walked toward the door. "What are you doing in the laundry
room?"

"That Sassy girl dropped by with the quilts you ordered.
They're not going to wash themselves, and you can't put a new
quilt on the bed if they haven't been through soap and water."

They had ordered all of their quilts from Wendy, the owner
of the new quilt shop in town, the Sassy Seamstress.

They watched silently while Winnie left through the side
door. Janice took a deep breath. "Can we afford someone else
doing our housekeeping right now?"

Tess shook her head. "Not really."

They both turned to LuAnn, who was still staring at the
door where Winnie had just exited. She bit her lip as she often
did during times of reflection.

"What are you thinking, Lu?" Tess asked.

"Well, there's a lot of work to do getting the rooms on the
third floor ready for guests and the fourth floor ready for us.
We still have to look for furniture for the third floor, not to
mention anything we're not bringing from our own homes for
our suites. And you know once the third floor is finished,
which shouldn't be too much longer since James has been
caught, we'll be able to get the inspection done and might be
able to start accepting guests."

"So what are you suggesting?" Janice asked, suddenly quaking on the inside as LuAnn ticked off all the items they still had to purchase.

"Obviously," Tess said, "she wants to hire Winnie full time a month before we planned."

LuAnn nodded. "How much would that cost us?"

Tess shrugged. "I don't know off the top of my head. But I'll grab my calculator and crunch some numbers. It might stretch the budget pretty tight, but it might pay off in the end if we can cut back elsewhere...?" Her voice trailed upward in an unspoken question.

Dread hit Janice, and, before her friends even turned toward her, she knew exactly where they could cut back. She sighed. How could she say no? "The baby grand?"

"Not if it means too much for you to give it up, Janice."

The compassion in Tess's voice touched Janice, and she felt her eyes burn with tears that she would not release. This was not the time to let emotions manipulate the situation. Of all the necessary pieces they still needed, the large ticket item they didn't absolutely need was the piano. Shoving down her disappointment and forcing her pastor's wife smile, Janice swallowed, not so hard they could see it was difficult to speak. *Not my will, Lord.*

"Of course it doesn't mean too much for me to give up. Let's scratch it for now."

Reaching across the table, LuAnn covered Janice's hand. "I promise we'll make this up to you, dear one. As soon as we are

up and running and get our books in the black, the first purchase will be your piano."

Janice knew better. There would always be one thing or
another that would take precedence over a silly addition like a
piano. She nodded. "Don't worry about it. We can put a nice
accent table there and maybe another wing chair."

Janice spent Saturday at Stacy's, where the dust had accumulat-
ed, laundry had piled up, and three carry-out containers, including a leftover pizza box, cluttered the refrigerator. Her grandson
needed a home-cooked meal and a clean house. She didn't blame
her daughter. Being a single parent had to be one of the hardest
jobs there was, but she felt guilty that she'd been so neglectful the
last couple of months. She hadn't been present enough, and the
house reflected that neglect. And that wasn't fair to Stacy.
After Lawrence passed away, the deal was, she'd move in with
Stacy until she found her own place, and she'd help out with
household duties and babysit Larry while Stacy worked. And
she'd done that faithfully until LuAnn moved to Marietta and
the whole crazy idea of opening the inn came about.

Lord, what have I done? Is this truly Your will for me?

Neither of her children were too keen on the idea. Even
her church friends had stopped calling to ask her to lunch or
just to stop over for coffee. She just hadn't been available for
much of anything except the Inn Crowd.

A smile touched her lips as she sprayed furniture cleaner and wiped down the bookcase. The lemon scent made her happy and the darkening cloth confirmed her decision to forgo a shopping trip with the girls to Athens, where they hoped to find an affordable antique sleigh bed for the Moonlight and Snowflake room on the third floor. Having woken up early that morning, Janice was determined to make the place spit-spot before Stacy got out of bed and to have a good breakfast ready for the three of them. She finished dusting, sweeping, and mopping, and cleaned out the refrigerator all before eight thirty, when Larry stumbled into the kitchen shoving his round glasses on his face.

"Smells... different," he said lifting his nose for a whiff of the air.

"That, my little man, is what a clean house smells like." She kissed his head and nudged him to a kitchen chair, then poured him a glass of milk to keep him occupied. "Drink this while I whip us up some breakfast."

"Can we have french toast?"

With a wink and the joy rising inside her chest, Janice nodded at her grandson. "I think I can manage that. How about bacon?"

He nodded as he drank his milk. Then wrinkled his nose. "It's not chocolate."

"No, it's not."

"Can I have chocolate in it?" He smiled up at her, showing off a milk mustache. What grandmother could say no? But first...

"Magic word?" She grinned at him.

"Please!" he said, grinning back.

She located the chocolate syrup and a spoon and stirred as the milk turned color. "There, now you enjoy that while I fix your breakfast."

The bacon sizzled at one end of the griddle, and french toast browned at the other.

Stacy wandered into the kitchen barefoot, wearing pajamas and her father's ratty bathrobe. She'd nearly had a fit when she noticed the old thing in a pile of throwaways while Janice was packing up the parsonage.

"Smells good in here," she said, walking straight to the counter for a mug of coffee.

"Nana said that's the smell of a clean house."

Stacy turned accusing eyes on Janice. "Well, I haven't exactly had time to do a lot of cleaning."

Cringing inside, Janice slid a spatula under the last of the french toast and added it to the pile on the platter. Next she placed the bacon on another platter and turned off the griddle. Typically, the best thing to do in situations like this was count to ten before she answered and made things worse. This time, she counted to twenty and added a prayer for help. Why must Stacy always twist her words?

"That's why I stayed home today, Stace," she said calmly as she set both platters on the table and took her seat in front of the place she'd set for herself.

"Well, I'm sorry I'm so dirty that you had to drag yourself away from your exciting life to do drudge work."

Exciting life? Janice opened her mouth to give her daughter a lesson in reality, when she noticed Larry. The little boy's eyes were enormous as he glanced first at his mother, then at Janice for her response. There was not one chance that Janice was going to get drawn into an argument in front of her grandson, so she bit her tongue and put two slices of bacon and two pieces of french toast on Larry's plate. "Eat up, buddy."

He grinned, as though the sight of fluffy french toast and crispy bacon made everything better again. If only a good hearty breakfast was all it would take to fix the rift between her and her daughter, whatever it was. Then a thought hit her. Was it possible that Stacy was resentful of all the time Janice spent at the inn and with LuAnn and Tess? Did she miss her mom?

She studied, Stacy, who stared hard at the food on the table as though trying to decide whether her stubbornness outweighed her appetite. Apparently, her stomach won as she reached out with her fork and grabbed several slices of bacon and a couple of pieces of toast. Janice forced herself not to smile and helped herself to breakfast, though her own appetite had faded.

Actually, it felt pretty good to think that her daughter wanted to spend more time with her. She should have recognized the signs earlier in Stacy. She'd witnessed the same reaction plenty of times when her daughter was younger and Lawrence was never home because of his work at the church.

It would still be a few weeks at least before the fourth floor was finished, so she couldn't fix the situation just yet. And she still wasn't entirely convinced she should even stay in the venture. She thought about the funds she'd already sunk into the project. She couldn't very well expect her friends to pony up a refund when they had counted on her one-third contribution. She stared at a beam of light filtering in through the gap between the two curtain panels above the sink, noting the motes of dust floating in the sunlight, and silently prayed for the right answer.

CHAPTER EIGHT

Janice couldn't remember a better, brighter Sunday morning to attend church. It was warm but not too warm as she walked from the car to the air-conditioned building.

Pastor Ben and his wife, Paige, met her as she walked into the foyer. They were either Hollywood-worthy actors, or the warmth of their greeting was more genuine and welcoming than she had dared expect or hope for considering her absences of late.

"Mrs. Eastman," Pastor Ben said, reaching out to hug her tightly, the way Stu often did. "It's so good to have you here."

"Th-thank you," she replied, as she took an awkward step back. "It's good to be here. Such a lovely Lord's day."

Paige, bubbling with a personality that drew a person right in, hooked her hand through the crook of Janice's arm and nudged her gently toward the sanctuary. "Do you want to come sit with me?" she asked. "I always feel a little strange, sitting on that big pew all alone while Ben is up front. Did you feel that way?"

A small, sympathetic smile tipped Janice's lips as she recalled their first few months as newlyweds and new pastors of Christ Fellowship. She nodded. "I remember the feeling all too well."

"Mrs. Eastman . . ." Paige began.

"*Psst.* Janice, over here!"

The two voices mingled, and she turned to find Tess and LuAnn sitting midway up the sanctuary. She turned and smiled at the new pastor's wife. "Looks like my friends saved me a seat. But I could..."

"Of course not. You join your friends." She laughed. "I guess I'd better get used to sitting alone."

Janice pressed her palm against the slender hand still holding to her elbow. "It gets easier. Until the kids come along." She grinned. "Then you have to decide how to keep them quiet so they don't disturb anyone or risk leaving service and disrupting that way." And Paige would be criticized either way. Janice remembered well.

With a squeeze of her hand, Paige let go but took Janice by surprise by leaning and whispering in her ear, "I might just have an announcement about that coming up soon."

Ah, that explained the new glow shining from her face. A genuine joy rose up in Janice for them, and she grinned as Paige pressed her finger against her full, glossy lips. "It's a secret so far."

Janice winked. "Mum's the word." Reaching forward, she pulled her into a quick embrace. Was it her imagination or were there tears in Paige's eyes when she pulled back?

"Janice!"

She turned and nodded at Tess, as Paige patted her arm and moved on.

Tess scooted over, leaving a space on the seat next to her. Janice noticed that she was still wearing the walking boot

Stuart had given her, but she must have been doing better to be out at church, despite yesterday's outing.

"What was that all about?" LuAnn asked, leaning forward and turning her head from her place on Tess's other side.

"What?"

"The pastor's wife being your new best friend." She leaned closer and dropped her tone even more. "I thought you said you didn't trust anyone who smiled that much."

Janice's face warmed at the memory. She had said that. She'd felt Paige's sweet positivity couldn't possibly be genuine and it irked her that all of the congregants who had been around as long or almost as long as she and Lawrence had been there, insisted that she reminded them "so much" of Janice when she was a young pastor's wife. She waited for the familiar resentment to rise at the thought, but it didn't come.

Janice shrugged at LuAnn's comment. "I might have misjudged. I'm human, you know."

LuAnn smiled and patted Janice's hand.

"Good morning, ladies."

Gratefully, the interruption brought that uncomfortable twist of conversation to an abrupt halt. The three of them turned to see Robin dressed in a light, black dress with a red, short-sleeved half cardigan.

"Oh, goodness gracious goat," Janice said. "Robin, honey, I almost didn't recognize you..." She was going to say "outside of your construction clothes," but quickly recovered. "...with your hair down and all curly like that. You're simply beautiful."

"You clean up nicely," LuAnn said with a smile.

Robin chuckled. "Thank you. I can when I need to."

Tess had a painted-on smile, clearly still convinced there was more to Robin than met the eye. "Would you like to join us?"

Motioning toward a pew a few rows back on the other side of the aisle, Robin shook her head. "I'd love to, but my mother is here from Toronto and that's my sister with her. They're saving my seat. I just saw you sitting up here and wanted to say hi."

With a little trepidation, Janice noted Isaiah was also sitting there with an obvious space between him and the older of the two women. She supposed he was saving that spot for Robin.

"Oh," she said. "Isaiah invited you?"

"Yes, ma'am." Robin's dimples deepened as she smiled from her eyes to her full lips.

Well, rats. If Robin and Isaiah found each other, where did that leave Stacy? And what about Isaiah asking for Stacy's number? Had he decided not to call, or had Stacy shot him down?

The music started, and Robin smiled. "I'd better go find my seat. I'll see you tomorrow if I don't see you after church."

Surprisingly, Pastor Ben had grown in his ability to present the Word over the last few weeks. Janice thoroughly enjoyed his message entitled "God is in Control." His text was from Isaiah 41: "So do not fear, for I am with you; do not be dismayed, for I am your God. I will strengthen you and help you; I will uphold you with my righteous right hand." The words honed in on a place in her heart that held the most anxiety—namely the financial pressures she would face if they couldn't make a go of the inn within a reasonable amount of time. And his secondary scripture, from Proverbs, spoke to her situation with Stacy: "Trust in the Lord with all thine heart and lean not unto thine own understanding." All in all, by the time Pastor Ben shook her hand at the door, pulling her in for a quick hug, Janice felt better than she had in weeks.

The sun had gathered its rays and seemed to concentrate them right on the parking lot by the time they reached their cars, parked only a couple of spaces apart. The temperature was at least ten degrees higher than when Janice had arrived an hour earlier.

Normally, she'd be eager to get back to Stacy's, kick off her shoes, change into comfortable clothes, and doze to a movie on the Hallmark channel. But despite the August scorcher, the sky was beautifully blue with puffs of white do-nothing clouds, and she felt so good, she agreed without hesitating when LuAnn suggested lunch at River Town Grill.

"You've got to see the sleigh bed we got for the Moonlight and Snowflakes room, Janice," LuAnn said as they settled into a table and ordered drinks. "I just couldn't believe it when we walked into the shop. It was a consignment store and not even specifically antique."

"More like a junk store." Tess grinned. "Tell her who suggested we go in there and who didn't want to."

LuAnn rolled her eyes. "Fine. We had looked at every antique furniture store in Athens."

"She was about ready to give up," Tess said.

"Because I was the one pushing the wheelchair all day." She smiled at Tess. "Not that I minded."

Tess continued. "Anyway, I saw this little hole-in-the-wall thrift-store type of place. It was just awful, but I felt drawn to it."

"She's not kidding, it was awful." LuAnn gave an exaggerated shudder. "You should have seen it, Janice. I took one look at the outside and told Tess there was no way that place had anything we could possibly use."

"But you never know, so I didn't see the harm in looking."

Janice grinned at the way the two of them were talking over each other just like they always did when they were girls together in college. She had to admit there was something comforting in realizing these friends she'd been blessed with for four decades of her life really were the same at the core of who they were as when they all became friends. Was she the only one who wasn't the same?

She shook off the thought, refusing to dwell on it, as LuAnn continued their tale. "Maisie, the woman at the shop, was so kind. But sort of unkempt, if you know what I mean."

Tess snorted. "That's putting it mildly. I'd bet my last dollar she's a hoarder."

"I think her building is just too small for the amount of inventory she has."

"How is that not being a hoarder?"

Janice couldn't hold back a giggle. They were forced to stop talking when the server arrived with their iced tea, and they ordered burgers and fries. They thanked her and she smiled, promising to be back in a jiff with their food.

"Anyway," LuAnn said when the server had returned to the kitchen, "turns out, her mother passed away many years ago and she had this bed, which had been handed down from her grandmother. Handcrafted by the woman's grandfather. Maisie, the woman in the shop, that is. When I asked about a sleigh bed—not really thinking she'd have a thing we wanted—she said, as a matter of fact, she did have one."

"And put down her cigar—I kid you not." Tess wrinkled her nose. "I could barely breathe, it was so smoky in there. I'm surprised she hasn't ignited the whole place before now and collected insurance money."

"Well, thankfully, she hasn't. Because the bed frame is made of solid oak! It's so sturdy."

Janice gasped as Tess pulled out her phone and showed her the photographs. Even though it was scarred and covered with dust, this was clearly the bed they had been searching for. "This is perfect. Was it very expensive?"

The look that passed between LuAnn and Tess sent a wave of nervous dread through her. "How much?" she asked.

Suddenly, LuAnn grinned and named a price so obscenely low, Janice suspected for a second that she was surely joking.

"How can that be?" She frowned. "You didn't..."

"Didn't what?" Tess's voice rose in indignation. "Hoodwink that poor old lady? Of course not! We tried to give her four times the amount she asked for. She could sell it online to an antique dealer for that much, who would price it even higher. But she wouldn't even consider taking more."

LuAnn broke in. "Apparently, after her mother passed away, the house was left to Maisie and her brother—neither of whom ever married. They lived there together until he passed away a few years ago. Since then, she's been living alone. Her neighbor brought the sleigh bed over to the shop for her right after her brother died and…well, we won't tell this to our guests…he died in the bed! That's why she didn't want to keep it in the house."

"That's awful!"

"Awfully cheap." Tess sipped her tea, then set it down on the paper coaster. "But it wasn't like he didn't live a good, long life. He was eighty-eight when he died."

"Mercy," Janice said. "How old is Maisie?"

Tess shrugged. "Too old to be working in that shop, that's for sure."

"I'd guess she's in her nineties." LuAnn smiled as the server stood by the table holding their tray. "Boy you weren't kidding when you said you'd be back in a jiff." The server made sure they had everything they needed, then left them to their meal.

"Who wants to say the blessing?" LuAnn asked, glancing at Tess.

It was fair LuAnn hadn't looked to Janice. After all, she had been deferring that particular honor for so long, she probably hadn't said a prayer over one of their outings in ten years. "I will," she spoke up. She didn't wait for them to show surprise but closed her eyes, bowed her head, and said a quick prayer of thanksgiving.

"Well, okay, amen then," Tess said with a nod. "There's more good news about the hoarder lady." She dipped a fry in a puddle of ketchup and nodded to LuAnn while she popped it into her mouth.

"Maisie said she's selling the house soon because she doesn't have any descendants to leave it to," LuAnn said with a frown as she inspected her burger. "I thought I said no pickles." She shrugged and pulled off four slices. "She's decided to retire and live the rest of her life on the proceeds from the house. She's never lived anywhere but there and wants to rent an apartment. Something small and bright. Her words."

"She's got to be sitting on a gold mine with as old as it is," Janice observed.

"If it's been kept up," Tess said.

"Anyway," LuAnn continued, "we made an appointment to meet her next Saturday to go through the house and make offers on anything we might be able to use."

"That's fantastic!" Janice said. "Do you think she'll sell the other things as cheaply as the bed?"

"I hope so," LuAnn said. "If she does, we'll save enough money to pay Winnie's salary for months and still furnish several of the guest rooms. She said there are five bedrooms full of furniture, and she won't have some greedy antique dealer trying to get their greasy fingers on her memories."

Tess nodded. "That's not even the best part. Tell her, Lu."

"When the inn changed hands in 1913, the new owner auctioned off most of the furniture, and Maisie's family bought the bulk of it. The bed is just one piece of many she still has."

Janice felt her jaw drop. "That is so hard to believe."

Tess swallowed a bite of her burger and washed it down with a sip of her tea. "I believe God led us there. We've been praying about finances."

LuAnn nodded. "Plus, He helped us figure out the wiring situation, with Robin's help. So that puts us back on track for getting the third floor up and running in a couple of weeks with all the work they've already done on it."

"It still burns me up that we lost those days without the electricity just because of James."

"Don't look now," Janice said. "But he's heading over here."

Predictably, LuAnn and Tess followed her gaze. James, red-faced and eyes blazing, was marching their direction. Why on earth would he be angry with them? They hadn't fired him. Thorn had done that before they even got back to the inn on Friday. He'd called him immediately after Robin hooked up the wires on the circuit box.

"I won't have my reputation besmirched!" he said without so much as a greeting. His calloused finger shook as he pointed it at no one in particular, but all three of them in general.

Fear gripped Janice and she felt herself shrinking into her seat, wishing she was against the wall where LuAnn sat, rather than the one closest to the angry man.

Tess clearly felt no intimidation whatsoever. "Then I suggest you not defraud your customers by sabotaging your own work to keep yourself working longer."

His fist came down on the table inches from Janice's plate, rattling her silverware. She jumped and let out a yelp. But he no longer paid her or LuAnn any attention. His pointing, shaking finger was practically touching the tip of Tess's nose. And still, Tess seemed completely nonplussed by the confrontation, his close proximity, or the fact that he was leaning on his fist over their table. Janice's ears roared as he took a couple of deep breaths.

"Lady, I never liked you from the first, but you'd better know I didn't do a thing to my breaker box. I have a reputation in this town that started with my dad and his dad and I'm not going to see our family name tarnished over three old ladies and this stupid idea you have to run an inn you have no business running."

Janice didn't dare remind him that they went to school together. If they were old, what did that make him?

"You don't think we should be running the inn, James?" LuAnn asked, and Janice was imagining her writing down this encounter in her journal of suspects and clues. "Why is that?"

He stopped short, gathering in a breath as he straightened up. "There's better uses for that building than some lacy, flowery inn no one wants."

Tess sat up to her full height and glared at him straight on, while Janice shook from the inside out and all the way down from her head to her toes. From the corner of her eye, she could see the manager heading their way. Relieved, she noted that he looked like a bouncer and only hoped he didn't take too long to get over to the table before Tess got herself into an all-out brawl.

"Do you mean no one wants our inn here enough to say… disconnect wires or, oh, I don't know, plant some old bones?"

His gaze narrowed, but he didn't seem a bit surprised that Tess had mentioned the bones. A short laugh left him. "I'll be coming by to get the rest of my things tomorrow. And you three should be careful. You don't know who you have coming in and out of that place."

"What are you talking about?" Janice said, finally finding her shaky voice.

Tess waved her hand and scowled. "Oh, he's just trying to throw us off the scent."

"Lady, think whatever you want to think."

LuAnn leaned forward, suddenly wearing her suspicious face. "Speaking of who we do or don't have coming into our place, you should be informed that I have already spoken to Mr. Thornton and he has installed a deadbolt on the tunnel door, for now, so if you made a spare key, it won't work. Plus, we'll be boarding it up on the inside so no one can use it until we can figure out how to keep it secure for the inn and our guests."

During her diatribe, James's face had paled, then turned red as anger flashed in his eyes. "Now, listen here. I'm not going to sit by and let my family's name and good reputation be sullied just because you three have too much time on your hands and watch too much TV." He turned to Janice. "Why don't you ask your son what he was doing at the inn Wednesday night after dark? Oh, and by the way, it's not the only time I've seen him there at night."

Before any of them could respond to the ridiculous comment, the manager finally reached the table. "Is there a problem here?"

"Yeah," James said, sweeping the three of them with a scathing glance. "But nothing that concerns you." He brushed past the man and stomped out of the restaurant.

Shaken, Janice sat back in her seat, her appetite utterly gone. "What do you think he meant about Stu?"

"Don't even worry about him," Tess said, pressing her hand over Janice's.

But LuAnn had pulled her notebook from her bag and was writing fast.

"What are you doing?" Janice asked.

LuAnn looked up, slowly setting down her silver pen. "Writing down Stu's name on the list."

Janice gasped and shoved back from the table to stand, her legs shaking so hard at the hint of confrontation, let alone the real thing, that she thought she might drop. But she couldn't let this betrayal go unchallenged. "LuAnn Sherrill! You've known that boy since he was born. You know as well as I do that he wouldn't rob a grave and dump the bones in our inn if his life depended on it."

"Janice, honey," LuAnn said, "sit back down. You know I don't really think Stu's done anything nefarious."

Tess drew a deep breath and leaned forward. "People are looking at us."

Janice sat down slowly. "Stu would be so hurt if he thought you—either of you—believed there was one ounce of truth in that man's words."

"Okay, you two, listen," Tess said. "Lu, put Stu under 'persons of interest' rather than 'suspects.' Okay?"

Janice folded her arms across her chest. "That sounds like the same thing to me."

But Tess shook her head. "No, a person of interest is some-one the police don't really think had anything to do with a crime, but they still want to question even though they know it'll rule that person out as a *suspect*."

LuAnn scratched out Stuart's name under her *suspects* heading and added a new heading on the next page: *Persons of interest*. "Better?" she asked, her eyes earnest as she met Janice's gaze.

"I suppose. But I'm going to have a little talk with my son before I take the word of James Avery."

Janice wouldn't rest until her son's name was completely scratched out of that book.

CHAPTER NINE

When Janice returned to Stacy's after her eventful lunch, Stacy and Larry were lying down for Sunday afternoon naps. Deciding to follow suit, Janice went to her room and changed out of her church clothes into comfortable exercise pants and an oversized T-shirt. She crawled into bed but found herself staring at the ceiling, allowing her mind to wander back to James Avery's accusation.

Was it possible her son was trying to sabotage the inn's opening? He certainly had access to bones. Well, maybe not one-hundred-year-old bones. He *had* seemed awfully familiar with the layout of the basement the other day when he collected those remains and went straight to the back door, where he'd parked just outside the basement entrance. But how would he have gotten inside? Only Tess, LuAnn, and Janice had keys to the house. Except for Winnie, of course. The key that opened the front door also opened the kitchen door. But the basement door lock was more secure, and different from the other two.

But only the four of them could get inside with a key.

Well no, she realized. Thorn also had one, since he and his crew had started working overtime and coming in before seven each morning. That was five keys in existence that she knew of. The thought gave her stomach a tremor. Had someone else—

she still couldn't make herself picture her son stalking about doing who knew what—gotten hold of a key?

For the life of her, she couldn't imagine why anyone would dig up someone's bones and bring them to the inn. And if someone did just want to scare them—which worked in her case—or cause another delay, why not break in and do damage to the place?

She slid out of bed and went to her desk, where she pulled the secret photograph from the middle drawer. She had placed it in plastic and slipped it inside an envelope. Since she'd found the photograph, she'd spent two nights at the inn, and last night she'd watched Larry while Stacy went out to dinner and a movie with her friends.

She'd been waiting for the opportunity to study the photograph, and this was the first chance she'd had. She knew she should tell someone about the photo, but she just wanted to know more first. She pulled it out of the envelope. The woman was striking. Though the photo was an ambrotype, extremely old and cracked, it was obvious that the little girl was very light-skinned. Her curly hair, which flowed over her shoulders and was tied up with a bow, was light—almost blonde.

She turned the photograph over several times and noted writing on the back but couldn't make out the names. She grabbed a magnifying glass, studying it for a moment as fond memories of her husband sprang into her mind. Lawrence always loved collecting old rocks and arrowheads. He used the magnifying glass to study each one so he could sketch the different lines and colors. Larry reminded Janice so much of his grandfather that her eyes misted. They would've been quite the pair in their adventures. If only...

With a deep breath, she shoved away the thoughts, which would only make her sad, and held the glass over the back of the photo. It was still difficult to make out the writing. Almost impossible. The date was 18—something. But what was the rest? Sixty? She couldn't be sure. Maybe 1880 something. Of the names, she could make out a *C* on the first one, which she assumed was the woman's. And on the other, she was almost sure there was a *W.* There was another word, but it was too faded to even attempt to guess what it said. But this was a beginning. If she could figure out who was in the photograph, maybe she could solve the mystery of the bones.

Still looking at the photograph, she walked to her bed and climbed on top of the covers, propping on pillows against the headboard. She picked up a stack of papers from the night-stand and settled back with the journal of Prudence Willard. The woman was part of the Underground Railroad and helped many slaves escape by using the tunnels and hidden rooms inside the inn. The Inn Crowd had discovered her journal a couple of months ago. Before handing it over to Margaret Ashworth at the historical society for safekeeping, LuAnn had photographed each page and printed them each a copy.

Before she started reading, she decided to pray for guidance. *Sovereign Lord,* she began, *it would mean so much to me if You would help me solve this one.*

As soon as she invited God into the mystery of the photograph, guilt nearly overwhelmed her. She recognized conviction for what it was and took in a shaky breath. She had a decision to make: surrender this all to God and stop letting her pride cause her to keep the photograph from her friends, or be honest with them both and work together to solve the mystery, the way they had twice before.

Janice arrived at the inn later than Tess and LuAnn the next morning. After her behavior at the restaurant, she was having a hard time facing her friends, and her stomach churned with each step from her car to the porch. But both sat at the little breakfast table, a pot of coffee between them, and a third cup waiting for her.

Janice knew they wouldn't linger over coffee today. They planned to spend the day decorating the second-floor rooms and unpacking books in the sitting room for their guests to enjoy. And Tess's son-in-law, Michael, was driving to Athens, about an hour away, to pick up the sleigh bed for the Moonlight and Snowflakes room.

"Did you sleep okay, hon?" LuAnn asked, a concerned tone in her voice as she peered at Janice's face.

"Not as well as I'd have liked." She took the cup that Tess had just filled for her. "I dreamed about skeletons, and you know how I hate nightmares. They scare me. I lay there from four o'clock to six afraid to go back to sleep."

"I'm pretty sure they're supposed to scare you," Tess said, a tiny smile playing at the corners of her lips. "I know you don't think it helps, but I always tell myself there's nothing to fear but fear itself. In the light of day, you just have to forget all about it and focus on other things."

Easy for her to say. She hadn't seen the bones Janice found.

"Well, it's no wonder you're dreaming about skeletons," LuAnn soothed. "Considering..."

Janice sipped her coffee. Over the rim, she noted a look passing between her two friends and could guess that they were as nervous to bring up their unofficial investigation as she was. But there was indeed an elephant in the room that had to be addressed. The three of them had never let disagreements come between them, and she wasn't going to allow that to start now, just because the subject of the disagreement happened to be her son.

With a sigh, she set her cup down and included them both with a sweeping glance. "I guess you two are dying to know if I talked to Stuart, so I'll tell you both right now, I wasn't able to get in touch with him at all yesterday."

"And if you had been?" LuAnn asked.

"I do not believe for one starry second that Stu had anything to do with us finding those bones." She paused to sip again and bolster her resolve. "But I know how it looks, and the questions need to be asked." She reached into her purse. Pulling out a small, battery-operated crystal clock she'd brought from Stacy's house, she set it on the table.

LuAnn and Tess stared at it, waiting for her to explain.

"This looks like a clock, but it has a little camera in it. Stacy bought this when Larry was born and she had to leave him with me while she went to work."

Tess gasped in outrage and opened her mouth, but Janice held up a hand. "It wasn't like that. She trusted me." She couldn't help but smile at Tess's defense of her. "She just couldn't bear to leave the little guy, and I was awful at taking videos so she could see him throughout the day. So, we bought this. It's like a nanny cam only it goes on a mantel or cabinet. I'd set it wherever I had Larry in the house, and she could see him."

"Does Stacy want you to bring it here now for when Larry comes over?" Tess gave a rueful smile. "He does tend to disappear."

"It probably wouldn't be a bad idea," Janice conceded. "But it turns out, it didn't work well enough for her to see him like she wanted, so I just learned to use the phone video recorder."

"And where do you propose we use this?"

"Well, when I was looking for Larry on Thursday, just before I found the bones, I saw muddy chunks across the basement, like someone had walked around kicking off dried pieces of the stuff."

LuAnn nodded. "Winnie about had a cow over that mud." She lifted one eyebrow. "But wait, that was Wednesday, not Thursday. Remember, she had to take one of Brad's aunts to an eye appointment, so she took off the whole day Thursday. And she complained about having to sweep up the mud, so I know it couldn't have been what you found the next day. So, we do have someone coming into the inn . . ." She swallowed, and Janice could only imagine she was remembering James Avery's accusation about Stuart.

"It's likely just workers," Tess said. "I mean, what are the chances? Nothing's missing from upstairs."

"That we know of," LuAnn said. "Besides, Janice heard someone down there. That's why she went into the tunnel to begin with, right Janice?"

"Yes. Tess, you were standing at the top of the steps when I heard that scraping noise. Remember?"

"I do, now that you mention it."

Janice ran her finger over the beveled top of the crystal clock. "That's why I think we should put the clock down in the basement and see who's sneaking in."

LuAnn nodded. "I agree."

Tess shrugged. "If you ask me, it's a waste of time, but I'm on board. But just in case I'm wrong and there is something to all this basement stuff, I think we should keep it between us for now."

Janice lifted her eyebrows and leveled her gaze at her friend. "Meaning, I shouldn't give Stu a heads-up just in case James was telling the truth?"

Neither friend spoke. Janice didn't blame them after her outburst the day before. "Well," she said, "unless I see it, I will never believe my son capable of criminal activity. But in order to ease your minds, I agree not to say a word to anyone about the camera."

She hesitated, dreading the next thing she had to do. She lifted the photo from her purse, sliding the envelope across the table to LuAnn.

"What's this?"

"Something I found with the bones Thursday."

LuAnn pulled it out of the envelope and drew in a sharp breath as she handed it to Tess.

"This was with the bones?" Tess frowned.

"Yes." Janice's heart raced as she waited for her friends to give her a good piece of their minds for withholding this fantastic part of the story. "And I'm so sorry I didn't tell you two about it right off."

Tess was still frowning at the photo. She waved her hand toward Janice. "Oh, it's been so crazy. You probably just forgot."

"Or didn't you forget?"

She forced herself to meet LuAnn's gaze, then she shook her head. "I kept it from you on purpose. I thought maybe I could solve the mystery on my own, and you two would be impressed. It was silly. I'm sorry."

"We're always impressed with you, Janice," LuAnn said. "And of course you're forgiven."

Janice's eyes got misty as LuAnn squeezed her hand.

"Let's make a new pact," Tess broke in. "No one keeps this kind of important stuff from the other two from now on. Okay?"

LuAnn nodded. "And it's not like you kept it very long."

"It certainly does put a new spin on things, doesn't it?" Tess said.

"What do you mean?" Janice asked.

"Well, the bones alone could have just been someone trying to delay our opening by getting the authorities involved, not to mention the university's archaeology department, but I think including the photograph is a personal touch."

"So, someone wants us to figure out who she is?"

Tess shrugged. "It's possible."

Janice's phone buzzed, interrupting their discussion. "It's Stu," she said as she picked up and greeted him.

"Hi. Sorry I didn't get your messages until late last night. Is everything okay?"

And if it hadn't been? What if she'd been lying on the floor and couldn't get Stacy's attention?

"Everything is fine. With me, anyway."

"Well, Stacy's at her desk, so she's okay and she dropped Larry off at day care. So, what was so urgent you called me so many times yesterday?"

Irritation spread over her at his implication that he'd been too busy for his mother. "Well, it's something I need to discuss with you in person."

"That works for me. I was planning to call you this morning anyway."

Janice raised her eyebrows in surprise. Stuart had been so busy lately, it had been almost impossible to connect with him. She'd considered faking a cold so he'd have to see her in his office, if nothing else. "Oh? What do you need?"

"The archaeologist from the university is missing some bone fragments from the remains you found. She asked if it would be possible to come to the inn and look around in the tunnel."

"Hang on. Let me talk to the girls." Janice relayed the request to LuAnn and Tess.

Tess frowned. "The forensics team was all over there and pretty thorough."

Janice nodded and turned her attention back to Stuart. "Stu, do you think you should call Chief Mayfield and ask him what forensics dug up?" She giggled. "Get it? Dug up?"

He chuckled. "I already called Mayfield. They didn't come up with anything useful."

"Well, what makes you think the archaeologist will have better luck?" And why did he seem so interested in whether she did or not?

"Forensics was looking for crime scene information, Ma, not archaeological fragments. She'd really like to see the site for herself. You'd be doing me a favor."

Something clicked in Janice's head. The university was in Athens. Stacy said Stuart had been seeing a woman from there. Unless she missed her guess, that archaeologist's name was Avi.

She grinned. "Well, I don't see any reason she shouldn't come give the tunnel a sweep. There's no electricity down there though, so make sure she brings in a good flashlight."

"She has equipment for that sort of thing." His tone sounded lighter. "Thanks, Ma. She doesn't teach on Tuesdays. Will tomorrow work for you?"

"I suppose."

"Thank you. Her team will be there around nine or ten in the morning. Oh, I have to go. I have a patient."

"Wait...Stu." With a sigh, she set her phone down and lifted her gaze to her friends. They both looked at her, waiting for an explanation. "Stuart's girlfriend is the archaeologist."

Tess's eyebrows went up in surprise. "He told you that?"

Janice shook her head. "No, but putting two and two together, I'd say so. Mother's intuition and all that."

LuAnn chuckled. "Now we know why he got right to the bones and sent them off so quickly. He must really like this one."

"Seems likely," Janice agreed.

"What aren't you telling us?" Tess asked, her tone edged with no-nonsense.

"Apparently, she's not coming alone. She'll have a team with her." She took a breath and exhaled. "And they have equipment." She imagined the archaeological dig scene in *Jurassic Park*—which she never should've watched. She'd dreamed of Tyrannosaurus rexes and Velociraptors for months afterward.

LuAnn groaned. "They'll be traipsing in and out the front door bringing all kinds of attention to the inn."

Tess nodded. "Cat's out of the bag, I guess. We won't be able to keep the bones a secret now." She let out a sigh. "We need to figure this thing out soon."

"On the bright side," LuAnn said, her eyes suddenly filled with humor, "Stuart's finally bringing a girl to meet his mother."

November 1858

Soaked to the skin and covered in mud, Prudence and her two companions trudged up the steps of her home. For the past hour, as they circled and made sure they weren't being followed, the man had been carrying Cecille in his arms.

Prudence had been almost as worried about how Jason would react to her bringing a package home instead of to the Riverfront House as she had been about Cecille's birth pains. She didn't have to wait long for his reaction. Before she could reach for the door, it flew open and Jason stood on the threshold, his shotgun resting on his shoulder as he leveled both barrels at the white man.

"Who is this?" he demanded, never taking his eyes from Logan.

Logan showed no fear as he met Jason's gaze with a steely calm. "Kindly lower your weapon. You're as likely to shoot the woman as you are me." How on earth he stayed so calm staring into Jason's stormy eyes, Prudence couldn't imagine, but she admired him for it all the same.

"Dearest, may we come in, please? I shall explain everything, but this woman is going to give birth soon and we must lay her down."

"Prudence, why has thee brought this trouble into our home? Didn't we have an agreement?"

Nodding, Prudence reached out and lowered the gun barrel. "As I have told thee, Husband, I had no choice. Please step aside so that our guests may get out of the wet and cold."

Cecille moaned, adding emphasis to Prudence's request, and Jason relented, though there was no mistaking his anger.

Prudence led the way to the bedroom she shared with her husband. This would likely anger him as well, but as soon as he discerned the situation for what it was, he would understand and prove to be as generous as Prudence knew him to be. But first, she had to undress Cecille and get her into the warm bed.

"Set her in the chair while I make the bed ready for her to deliver and help her undress. Thee may go into the other room. Jason, will thee put the warmer in the fire? I am afraid Cecille is soaked to the skin and chilled to the bone."

"Thee are as well, Wife." His look was pointed, but he didn't object to giving up his bed.

"Yes, but I am not about to deliver a child."

Even as she said the words, she thought of her secret. She would have to tell Jason soon.

Perhaps a little longer, God?

The sooner she told him, the sooner he would demand, as was his right, that she cease her participation in helping runaway slaves.

With the door closed behind the men, Prudence turned to Cecille, who had not uttered a word thus far. The agony on her face indicated she would likely give birth soon. Prudence pulled a fresh nightdress out of the wardrobe and noticed that next to the cabinet Jason had prepared her wash basin with fresh water and towels so she could wash before bed. A wave of love filled her at his consideration.

"Thee will feel better after these wet things are off and thee is snug in bed."

Cecille nodded. "Yes, ma'am." With Prudence's help, she undressed. Prudence left her to the wash basin and towels and slipped from the room to check on the men and the bed warmer. Jason had built up the fire and the front of the house was cozy.

Glancing around, she saw that Logan was absent.

"He's gone outside to gather more water to wash himself," Jason said through tense jaws.

"That was good of thee," she said quietly. She pulled the warmer from the fire and wrapped it.

The lantern glowed brightly on the mantel, and a moment of concern filled her. If someone came by in the night looking for them, a burning lantern would most certainly be suspicious this time of night.

Jason reached for the lantern, blowing out the flame as though he'd read her thoughts.

He touched her arm to stop her before she could walk away. "Explain thy actions. Does thee not realize what thee hast done?"

"I have done what I must. Thee would have done the same." A deep groan reached them from the bedroom. "Please, Husband. I must go."

They heard the deep sound of male voices outside, followed by heavy boot steps coming up the porch stairs.

Fear gripped Prudence. One of the voices was unmistakably that of Logan. Had Jason been right? Had her trust in this man brought them all to their doom?

CHAPTER TEN

Janice, Tess, and LuAnn spent the morning putting books into the floor-to-ceiling bookcases. They had two cases filled from their own libraries, donations from friends, and some estate sale finds, and at least that many more books waited in boxes to be put away.

The day before Tess's son-in-law had insisted on bringing the boxes in from the storage shed. "Michael is worth his weight in gold," Janice said, sliding in her last book.

She climbed down from the ladder, relieved her turn was over. Knowing her fear of heights, LuAnn had offered to be the official ladder person while the other two handed her the books, but Janice refused to let LuAnn do all the hard work. Since she'd braved her fear of the dark and gone into the tunnel, she'd decided she was tired of fear holding her captive. And with Tess's ankle still not fit to climb a ladder, it fell to Janice and LuAnn.

"Michael really has helped us an awful lot," LuAnn mused. "Are we paying him for all the grunt work we force on him?"

"I've tried," Tess said. "He's too stubborn."

"Ladies?"

At the sound of a female voice, they glanced toward the door.

"Robin!" LuAnn said. "Come in, honey."

She walked in tentatively and kept her gaze averted.

"Everything okay?" Janice asked.

"I just... Is there something you three need to tell me? I—I think you did something Friday, but I don't know how to ask."

LuAnn and Janice exchanged a guilty glance, and Janice's heart rate rose rapidly. Had Robin's neighbor finally realized there was no possibility that she and LuAnn could be her mother and sister?

"You just need to sit down and spit it out," Tess said. Clearly, she still suspected the young woman of being involved in, if not behind, the entire grave-robbing mystery.

Robin dropped onto a chair. "I just... Okay. I went to the city utility office to pay my electric bill during my morning break. Only..." She gathered in a deep breath. "This is so awkward. The woman behind the counter told me someone already paid it. She wouldn't tell me the name of the person, but I think I can guess."

Relief washed over LuAnn's and Tess's faces, and Janice was pretty sure that her own expression mirrored her friends'.

"I can tell by your reactions that you're the guilty parties," she said. She reached into her backpack and pulled out a couple of bills. "I-it's not the whole amount. I was going to try to pay half this week and half next."

Compassion spread across Janice's chest. "You put that away, honey. It was our pleasure to do it for you."

"But you don't even know me."

Tess limped over to the chair and dropped onto the ottoman directly in front of her. "You did save our bacon by figuring out the wiring problem."

"But that's just my job." Her eyes flashed a little. "I couldn't let that jerk take advantage of you."

"You took care of our electricity so we took care of yours. It's as simple as that." LuAnn's voice lilted as though she'd just thought of the most brilliant explanation. And it would have been if Robin weren't a little brilliant herself.

"But you paid my bill Friday morning, according to the woman at the office. I didn't find the wires disconnected from the box until around lunchtime."

Tess patted Robin's knee. "Let's not worry about it anymore."

"But how did you even know it was overdue?" Just their luck, this woman was a thinker. "They aren't allowed to give out private information."

LuAnn gathered a breath and sat in the chair next to Robin's. "We saw your bill."

Janice smiled at her. "Honey, you need to be careful about leaving that bag of yours open."

Robin's face deepened in color. "Oh, no! My disconnect notice fell out? I'm usually so careful to close my pack when my laptop is in there." Robin furrowed her brow, and Janice couldn't help but notice how pretty she was even when she wasn't smiling. "I truly don't feel right letting you pay my bill for me." She smiled. "I've been paying my own way since I was eighteen."

It was almost too hard to fathom that Robin could be behind this whole thing. Janice would almost have believed Stuart to be the culprit before she could believe it of Robin.

"Well, if you ever need any help moving things around, just give me a call," Robin said. Hesitating, she held out the money once more. "Are you sure you won't let me pay you back? It feels so wrong to let someone I barely know pay my bill for me."

Tess covered her hand and pushed it back. "Keep it. We wanted to do it."

"I don't know how to thank you."

"You can help me up from here," Tess said. "I don't know what I was thinking, sitting on this thing."

Robin stuffed the money back into her bag and made a point of zipping it shut before she stood, holding out her arm for Tess to grab on to. "How is the ankle?" she asked.

Tess grimaced, steadying herself with Robin's arm. "Better than it was, but still too weak to be on it for long."

"If you need help with anything at all, please don't hesitate to ask. It's not like I have much of a life outside of work." She slung her pack over her shoulder and smiled at all three of them. "And speaking of that, I'd better scoot before Thorn fires me."

"We wouldn't let him," LuAnn said, standing alongside her.

Robin gave her a quick hug. "I'm not sure what I've done to deserve you three angels. But I promise I'll make it up to you, somehow."

Tess started to sway, and grabbed on to the back of the chair for support. "Just keep those men on schedule so we can open our inn soon."

"You got it." Robin's dimples deepened, and she saluted before leaving the room.

LuAnn grabbed her purse from the table between the two chairs. She reached inside and pulled out her keys. "I have a copy of Prudence's journal locked up in the office. What do you say we go over to the tearoom and have lunch? Maybe we can find a reference to the woman and girl in the photograph."

A half hour later, they sat in a corner booth at their favorite restaurant in walking distance of the inn. They waited for the server to bring their orders before pulling out the photograph and the photocopied journal pages.

Tess squinted as she peered closely at the writing on the photo. "I can't make out any of this."

"The first letter of the first name is *C*," Janice said. "And I'm pretty sure the first letter of the second name is *W*. The date is either 1860-something or 1880-something."

LuAnn riffled through the pages. "The journal starts in 1854, so that eliminates the first pages. Okay, 1860. Prudence's son, Moses, is a year old."

"Starting in 1860 assumes that this photograph was taken here in Marietta. Would a former slave have taken a photo like this before the Civil War was over?"

They remained silent as, clearly, all three came to the same conclusion. LuAnn brought some of the pages forward. "That's a good point. We don't even know if Prudence ever saw this photograph."

"The only thing we have to go on is that the bones we found in the tunnel were left there for us to find," Tess said, "and it stands to reason that those, at least, are the remains of someone who died locally and a long time ago."

"But we have no idea where the photo is from."

"Here's an entry from 1859. 'Little Chloe clung to my skirt until I was forced to pull her into my arms and carry her the rest of the way to RH. I learned her mother died of a gunshot wound on their journey from Georgia. Abigail will raise her. Her own little ones were sold away from her years ago. I pray God will give her strength. She is quite old to be raising a little one. I was tempted to beg Jason to let me adopt her. But the risk is much too great. Both for the child and us.'" LuAnn looked up and shook her head. "That wouldn't be our woman and child."

Janice glanced up as the door opened. Robin walked into the tearoom alone. "Look."

Tess and LuAnn sat across from Janice with their backs to the door. They turned.

"I know what you're both thinking," Tess said, "but if we invite her over we'll have to put this away."

"We should anyway," LuAnn said. "We don't want her to overhear us discussing any of this. We haven't officially cleared her as a suspect, although I'm leaning toward Janice's feelings about her." She gathered the pages and stuffed them and the photograph into the accordion folder she'd brought them in.

Janice wanted to ask for the photo, but refrained as Robin walked up to the table.

"Looks like we had the same idea." Robin smiled and her dimples pitted her cheeks.

"Thorn sent you on to lunch when you'd just been on a break with us?" Tess said.

"I offered to work the first ten minutes to make it up, but he told me I wouldn't be much good to him if I was weak from hunger." She giggled.

"Will you join us?" Janice asked.

Robin's eyes clouded but only for a second. "Sure, I'd love to."

Janice almost felt sorry for asking. Robin clearly would have preferred to sit alone. She probably wanted to read or use the teashop's Wi-Fi but was too polite to refuse after they'd paid her electric bill. Janice could think of no way to rescind the invitation without seeming rude.

But maybe this was a good thing. Like Tess said, Robin hadn't been cleared as a suspect yet. Even if it was hard to imagine her being behind the bones or the photo, maybe they could use this time to learn more about her.

Robin ordered a basket of chicken strips, potato wedges, and a large Caesar salad on the side, with the homemade dressing the tearoom was gaining a reputation for. She had ordered a meal large enough for a grown man, it seemed to Janice.

Apparently, she noticed the looks of surprise on the friends' faces. She grinned. "I can out-eat anyone I know. My mother always said she had to work two jobs just to feed me."

"If you could bottle your metabolism, you'd be as rich as the president." Tess crunched a homemade chip, and her eyes glinted with humor.

Robin laughed. "I hear that all the time. I'm always moving."

Dying to learn more about Robin, Janice went for it. "How did you get into the construction business?"

"Necessity." Robin turned to Janice. "I needed a job and Mr. Thornton needed someone else on the crew, and for some reason he decided to give me a chance."

Tess sniffed as she set her tea glass on the table. "Well, I know he's glad he did, after the electrician fiasco."

"I take it you aren't from around here, then?" Janice drew the conversation back to collecting information. Wasn't that what they were trying to do, after all? "You mentioned yesterday at church that your mother and sister were visiting from Toronto?"

Robin nodded and reached out to run a finger down the moisture collecting on the outside of her glass. "That's where I grew up. But my sister actually moved here about a year ago. We've both always been intrigued with the area. She applied for and got a position at the university in Athens."

It was pretty clear she wasn't very interested in continuing this line of conversation, but from years of unofficially counseling women, Janice knew that a little nudge was usually all it took to encourage someone to open up, even when she didn't want to. "What sort of work did you do in Canada?"

She shrugged, resigning herself to the topic. "A little bit of everything. I worked as a server and bartender for a lot of years while I took classes. I even did plumbing once."

"And what is your degree in?" Tess asked. She perked up at anything that smacked of academia.

"I didn't actually graduate. The money wasn't there, and, unlike my sister, I wasn't able to hold on to any scholarships. But I was studying history. Specifically, the history of runaway slaves who made it to Canada in the 1800s. That's part of the reason this town fascinates me so much. The underground activity around the river."

LuAnn leaned in. "We've been doing a bit of studying on that topic ourselves."

"LuAnn is our resident historian," Janice said, proudly. "She taught American history for years."

Robin raised her eyebrows with interest. "Oh?"

Only Tess seemed a bit off as she narrowed her gaze, suspicion clouding her eyes again. "Quite a coincidence how you ended up working on an inn that used to be a stop on the Underground Railroad."

Janice sent a warning look to her friend. After all, if they wanted to get information, they had to use covert interrogation techniques, not be hostile and suspicious. Like her mother used to say, "You catch more flies with honey than vinegar." "Sometimes providence is masked in coincidence."

"Well, to be honest with you," Robin began, "like I said, I'm fascinated with the town's history. But part of the reason I came to Marietta is because I knew about the Riverfront House. My sister wanted me to stay with her in Athens, but this is where I wanted to be. The very first day I got to town, I met Isaiah Wimber, right here in this shop, as a matter of fact. I came in to apply for a job, and I overheard him mentioning to the owner that Thorn was looking for more workers for the crew to renovate the inn. So I asked how to apply for a job. And the rest is history." She smiled but not fully with her eyes, which wasn't what Janice had come to expect.

Tess still didn't seem convinced. "What made you think you were qualified to do construction?"

This time, Robin's smile showed her dimples and flashed in her eyes. If she noticed that she was being interrogated, she didn't let on. "Habitat for Humanity. When I was sixteen, they chose my mom for one of their houses." Her expression softened even more. "It made such a difference for us that I got involved in the very next project, and I've helped build twenty homes since then."

Her obvious sincerity seemed to draw Tess in and shut down her skepticism. "That's remarkable."

"Well, I never thought I'd be doing it for a living, that's for sure. I feel almost guilty taking a paycheck for doing the work I've been volunteering for half my life."

LuAnn swallowed hard and cleared her throat. "So, Robin, how long will your mother and sister be in town?"

"Oh, they just stayed the weekend. My sister had to get back to work, and Mom's a lot more comfortable at my sister's apartment than mine. She'll be back and forth for the month she's here, though. We recently discovered," she said with a lilt in her voice and a dimply smile, "that we have distant relatives across the river in Williamstown. Of course, we haven't met them and I'm too chicken to just walk up to the front door and knock, but it's been interesting to research all of the history surrounding this area."

And just like that, Tess's radar pricked back up. "So, you didn't come to Marietta just because of the Riverfront House?"

Robin laughed. "No. Having distant relatives nearby definitely weighted my decision toward this area, and my sister's decision, of course. We grew up hearing stories about the inn. It's probably what captured my imagination when I was a kid and made me want to know more about the Underground Railroad. A lot of runaways who came through Ohio ended up in Toronto, including one of my ancestors."

"I'd be interested in that part of history from a different perspective," Janice said. "We hardly hear stories about the escaped slaves after they made it to Canada. Even fiction stories usually end with them reaching freedom."

"That's exactly why I decided to study more about it. I'd love to write a book someday featuring one slave from the time she escaped the plantation all the way to freedom and what her life looked like after she reached Canada." Robin shrugged. "You know, how did she build her life? Is there a huge family of descendants who wouldn't be here today if not for that one person's courageous escape from slavery?" She blushed, as though she realized she'd allowed her passion to show to virtual strangers. "Anyway, it's a dream."

Janice patted her hand. "It's a very good dream. And one that I've never seen written about in much detail. I hope you do it."

"So do I."

Tess insisted on paying the bill for everyone, including Robin, who protested but ultimately gave in. The four of them walked back to the inn together. When Robin returned to the third floor, the three friends went into the living room to unload more books.

"Well?" Tess said. "What do we think about her?"

Janice smiled. "She's charming."

"I'm pretty sure that's not what Tess is talking about, Janice."

As realization dawned, Janice planted her hands on her hips, leveling her gaze at her suspicious friend. "How can you possibly still think Robin had anything to do with any of this? She builds homes for poor people!"

"Actually," LuAnn said, "as much as I like her, finding out her past—"

"And the fact that she has family just over the bridge," Tess broke in.

LuAnn nodded. "Exactly. She seems like even more of a suspect than she was before."

Digging in her heels, Janice shook her head. "I don't want to believe it. And you heard her, those are distant relatives she doesn't even know. They may as well be the man on the moon. Besides, I still suspect James. He went through the tunnel, so he was obviously in the basement. Plus, he's a bully and seems like the type of person who would definitely dig up someone's bones."

"I think they call that an archaeologist—like your son's girlfriend." Tess snickered.

"Laugh all you want, but that James Avery is still at the top of my list."

"He is still a suspect," LuAnn reminded Janice and Tess.

The bell above the front door sounded, signaling someone's arrival. LuAnn glanced through the open doorway between the living room and entryway and nodded. "Speak of the devil."

James clomped into the house. "Hello!" he called. "Thorn!"

Thankfully, Thorn appeared immediately, before they had to greet the unpleasant man. He waved James up the steps.

"What do you suppose he wants?" Janice asked.

"He said he left some things here," LuAnn reminded her absently. "What is that on the floor in there?"

She walked from the living room to get a closer look. Janice followed and Tess, still limping, brought up the rear.

Janice bent to inspect whatever LuAnn had spotted. Then she gasped. "I knew it!"

"What?" Tess glanced over Janice's shoulder. "Oh. Would you look at that?"

That rotten James Avery had left a trail of dried mud all across the entryway from the door to the stairs.

CHAPTER ELEVEN

Livid! That was the word that came to mind as Janice stared at the chunks of mud. "I wish we'd thought to collect samples of the mud from the other day to compare with this."

"Well, we can collect some of this." LuAnn headed for the kitchen. "I'll be back."

"Hurry!" Janice said. "Before he comes back."

Tess pulled back the curtains and glanced out the window. "If this ankle didn't make me so slow, I'd go out to his truck and see what he's got hidden in that box."

Janice froze at her implication. She'd known Tess for too many years not to recognize her subtle hint. Shaking her head, she stepped back from her friend. "I'd die. You know I would."

"You're probably right. Besides," she said, dropping her volume, "here he comes."

He barely nodded as he stalked past them, and Janice was hard-pressed not to call the police on him right then and there. She barely registered LuAnn's return from the kitchen as she made a quick decision, drawing in a sharp breath as a sense of urgency filled her. She walked as fast as she could into the living room, grabbed their three purses, and rushed back to the entry. LuAnn stood with the bag of dirt, just as Janice shoved her purse into her arms.

LuAnn looked at the bag, then back to Janice. "What's going on?"

"Hurry and put that sample away," Janice said, fishing inside her purse for her keys. "Let's follow him again."

"That's more like it," Tess said. "Help me, so I can get out to the car faster."

LuAnn closed the seal on the plastic bag and shoved it into her purse. "I'll drive."

"No," Janice said firmly. "Last time you drove, and we lost him."

"And almost died," Tess piped in. "I'll drive."

"I'll drive." Janice wasn't taking any chances of losing him this time. "Get in my car."

Whether they were in agreement or just surprised by Janice's vehemence, Tess and LuAnn acquiesced.

By the time they got inside the car and all buckled up, James's truck still sat in the parking lot, emitting fumes. He glanced toward them, then looked away just as fast.

"Oh no, we've been made," Janice said.

"First of all, no we haven't. He's on his phone. Just ease out of the lot and wait for him along the street. He won't think twice about us following him. He never even mentioned LuAnn's crazy driving on Friday, so he obviously doesn't notice much."

"What's the second of all?" Janice asked. She kept his truck in view as she did as Tess suggested. "You said, 'first of all.'"

"Oh. Second of all, don't use phrases you learned from *Law and Order*. It sounds like you're trying too hard."

"Well, I thought he made us! What else was I supposed to say?"

"Stop arguing and pay attention," LuAnn said. "He's on the move."

Tess grunted. "You two are hopeless. Don't lose him, Janice. He's turning the other way out of the lot. Hurry, make a U-turn."

With direction reversal worthy of any TV crime show, Janice whipped the car around, narrowly missing a Vespa scooter.

LuAnn's hands white-knuckled the dash as she held on for dear life. "And you said my driving was bad!"

"Neither one of you should be on the road," Tess said. "From now on, I'm driving when we're following someone."

They followed James all the way to the edge of town. "Does James live out this way?" Janice asked.

"I don't know where he lives," Tess said, her voice ringing with just a little too much excitement. Janice wondered if she'd missed her calling when she became a teacher. Tess would've made a great detective. Like *Cagney and Lacey*. "Just keep following him."

He picked up speed and Janice pressed down on the gas pedal, matching him.

"Don't get too close," LuAnn warned. "We don't want him to notice us. Besides, he's kicking up dust with his tires, and I can barely see where we're going."

"I'm telling you," Tess said. "It's those dark sunglasses. We should get you a lighter pair."

"And get melanoma of the eyeballs? Not likely."

Suddenly, James's truck whipped off the road a few yards ahead of them. Janice gasped as he jumped out and waved his hat for them to stop.

"Well, that does it. He's made us for sure now."

"Should I pull over?" Janice's stomach churned, and fear gripped her at the thought of confronting him.

"You might as well," Tess said. "What could he do to all three of us?"

"Well...if he has a gun," LuAnn mused.

Easing her car over, Janice rolled down the window. She watched him, looking for a weapon that might end them all. "Need something, Mr. Avery?"

"Excellent voice control, Janice," Tess whispered from the back seat.

"Yeah, I need to know why you three crazies are following me. And I know you followed me the other day too, so don't deny it."

"I think you flatter yourself." Janice gave a short but much too high-pitched laugh. "Can we help it if you're going the same direction we are?"

"Don't hand me that. I have half a mind to call Mayfield and have you arrested for harassment."

Could he do that?

Tess leaned forward from the back seat and stared at him. "If anyone's harassing anyone, buster, you're harassing us."

Janice glared at the man who, only twenty-four hours earlier, insinuated her son was up to no good. "What do you think the police would say to you sneaking into the inn?"

His eyes narrowed dangerously. "Prove it, lady," he challenged.

Ha! He didn't deny it. As a matter of fact, that sounded like an admission as far as Janice was concerned.

Tess got right to the point. "We want to know what's in that box."

"We sure do, buster," LuAnn chimed in.

Janice wasn't so sure she and her friends were on the same page. She'd seen enough bones to last her a lifetime.

"What box?" James said. The sneer on his face did nothing to improve his grizzled looks.

LuAnn pointed. "The casket-looking thing in the back of your truck."

He looked confused as he turned to look at his truck, then turned back. "You mean my toolbox?"

"So *you* say," Janice said in the spirit of solidarity, though she was regretting her impulsive decision to jump in the car.

He shook his head, sweeping his arm out toward the truck. "Be my guest."

"Careful," Lu said low enough that only the three of them could hear. "He might just be trying to lure us out of the car so he can do away with us."

That thought had also crossed Janice's mind. "Do we really need to see what's inside that box?"

"Yes," Tess said. "And stop letting your imaginations run wild. We're in no physical danger."

"Well, ladies? You going to have a look before I leave?"

Janice hated the mocking tone of voice. She reached for the door handle. "Yes, we are."

"Are you sure about this, Janice?" LuAnn asked.

Not one bit. But she wasn't going to just sit by and let this man get away with a bluff. "Tess, stay in the car, in case we need to get away fast."

LuAnn and Janice walked slowly toward the truck. Janice's legs quivered, but she forced herself to stay strong. It had, after all, been her idea to follow him. And it was her son's good name she needed to clear.

Up close, it was easy to see that the wooden box wasn't large enough to be a casket. Since they'd first noticed the box on Friday, James had turned it in the truck so the length of the box fit within the width of the bed. Janice was beginning to get the sinking feeling that they were, in fact, looking at a toolbox as James had said. He grabbed onto a rope handle on one end of the box and pulled it all the way to the open tailgate.

A car coming the opposite direction slowed down and stopped just as James reached for the lid.

"Everything okay here, Mrs. Eastman?"

Janice looked closer and recognized Pastor Ben. "Oh, hi. Yes, everything's just fine. James was just about to let us look inside his toolbox."

He raised his eyebrows at the news. Janice saw no reasonable way to explain that they were just confirming that there were no more bones inside, so she left it right there in the dusty silence of the dirt road.

James cast a disparaging glance at Pastor Ben like he held the man in highest contempt. It was obvious he didn't care at all about Pastor Ben's opinion of the situation, and that just burned Janice up! He sneered. "Nothing to see here, Preacher."

"Thank you for checking on us." LuAnn offered a smile and a little wave. "The service was wonderful yesterday."

Pastor Ben smiled and thanked her, but his eyes looked troubled. "James, will we see you over at the church one day this week?"

"Not likely," he growled. "Not much for religion."

"As much as I'd love to have you come to a service," Ben replied, "I meant to finish putting in the motion lights above the doors. You were going to come back last week."

"Oh, yeah. Sorry," he muttered. "I'll get over there tomorrow."

"Great, we'll look forward to seeing you."

"Sure."

"See you ladies next Sunday." Pastor Ben waved and drove away slowly.

James reached out and lifted the lid on the box. At one end inside, a smaller tool container held the equipment, tools, and wires from his electrician job. The rest of the box held hammers, saws, a pickax—nothing but general tools someone would have around the house.

"You ladies satisfied?" His voice sounded awfully huffy but not as angry as before. "Can I go now?"

Well, there was certainly no point in detaining him any further. They weren't equipped to haul him into the police station. So the best they could do right now was be satisfied that he wasn't hiding bodies or bones.

Janice and LuAnn barely had time to get back into the car before James spun his tires and sped down the road, flinging dust in his wake.

"Rude!" Janice said, as she put the car in gear. As they drove back to town, they filled Tess in on the conversation and the rusty, weathered tools in the box.

"Slow down," LuAnn commanded. "Sixty miles per hour on this dirt road is not safe."

Janice eased off the pedal, just as lights flashed behind them and a siren screeched twice. "Oh, bother. Will you get my wallet out of my purse, Lu? I suppose he'll want to see my driver's license. And don't say one word of this to Stu and Stacy."

Tess leaned forward from the back seat. "Well, as long as we have a cop here, at least tell him about seeing James come out of the tunnel and about the mud on his boots."

"Good idea," Janice said, taking her wallet from LuAnn as she rolled down the window. Her nerves calmed a little when she recognized Randy Lewis standing over her. "Mrs. Eastman, do you know how fast you were going?"

"Yes, I do, as a matter of fact. LuAnn just informed me I was going sixty."

"Sixty-two."

She gave him a wobbly smile. "Well, what's a couple of miles per hour?"

He pursed his lips together, then heaved a heavy sigh.

Janice had no time for a scolding. "I had a good reason."

With a slight frown, he bent over to look inside the car. "Someone hurt?"

"Well, Tess twisted her ankle the other day when she stepped in a hole. But she seems better."

"Much better," Tess chimed in.

151

"So, you weren't rushing to the hospital?"

"No, we're all just fine. Thank you for asking."

"I see." He coughed.

It registered, then, that he was trying to find a good excuse not to give her a ticket. The gesture warmed Janice—especially since her own children were being such a trial these days. Randy had been in her Sunday school class, and she'd had her doubts about him at one time. But he'd apparently grown up just fine.

"How are Sharon and the boys?"

He smiled. "Great. We just found out we're having another baby in March."

"Oh, that's wonderful!" Janice said, genuinely thrilled for the couple.

He scribbled on his pad, ripped out the sheet, and handed it to her. "Now, Miss Janice, I'm going to let you off with a warning because I'm sure you didn't realize you were driving so fast, but ease off the gas pedal before you get yourself and those two killed. Okay?"

"I certainly will."

LuAnn nudged her. "Tell him about James!"

"Randy," she called out before he could reach his car.

He returned in a few long strides. "Yes, ma'am?"

"We think we know who left the bones in the inn." Well, she knew who did. If Tess and LuAnn didn't, they would as soon as the police got James to confess.

"You do, huh? With no concrete evidence? The department should just hire you three and do away with all that nonsense."

He chuckled at his own—very poor, as far as Janice was concerned—joke.

"It's called deductive reasoning and common sense," Tess spoke up, annoyance edging her tone.

Janice told him their reasons for suspecting James. "So, you see? There's obviously more here than meets the eye."

"Okay, ladies. I can see you're convinced. I'll tell you what, I'll pass this information along to the chief and see what he has to say about it."

"Good," LuAnn said. "If we can get this wrapped up sooner rather than later, we might get our inn open on schedule."

"I'll do my best." He smiled. "Drive safely, Mrs. Eastman, and keep the speed down."

Janice rolled up the window and turned to LuAnn, then Tess. "You think he'll tell Chief Mayfield?"

LuAnn shrugged. "He said he would, and if you can't trust the police, who can you trust?"

"Well," Janice said. She put the car in gear and eased back onto the road. "You didn't know him when he was younger. That boy could lie like nobody's business without blinking an eye."

Twenty minutes later, they found themselves back at the inn and settled around the kitchen table with three steaming cups of the most fragrant tea—a new blend Winnie was trying out.

"Lavender and peppermint in chai. A nice calming blend that'll pick you up at the same time."

"Exactly what we needed, Winnie," Tess said. "I'm not sure about the peppermint, though."

Winnie's sharp gaze landed on Tess, and Janice felt compelled to jump in. "But it does tingle the tongue." Though she had to agree with her friend.

LuAnn whistled and set her teacup back on the table. "It certainly does do that."

"What have you three been up to that you need a good calming tea in the afternoon?" Winnie said it nonchalantly as she wiped down the counter, but it was clear she was all curiosity.

"Oh, just driving around." One thing you could say about Tess, she had the best ability to tell just enough to be truthful without giving away a secret.

"Driving around, huh?" Winnie set a plate of muffins between them. "Try those. Lemon blueberry with just a hint of cinnamon."

"They look wonderful," LuAnn said, reaching for one.

"I have to say something to you three."

Janice's stomach filled with dread. Were the tea and muffins Winnie's way of warming them up for bad news? If Winnie quit, they'd be sunk.

She dropped into a chair next to Janice and clasped her hands on the table.

Tess swallowed a bite and dabbed at the crumbs on the table with her napkin. "Something wrong?"

"Well, I have to say, I worked for the aunts for years and never, once, in all that time was I ever as insulted as I have been today by you three."

Janice couldn't hold in a little gasp. She could see by the looks on Tess's and LuAnn's faces that they felt exactly the same way.

"What are you talking about?" LuAnn asked.

"Well, don't think I didn't notice you put a fancy little clock down in that dark old basement. And I can tell you, you're not fooling anyone. I can spot a camera a mile away. Now, you want to tell me why you think you can't trust me?"

The three of them started talking at once. "Winnie, that's not about you," Janice said, her voice rising above the other protests.

"No, of course it isn't," LuAnn reiterated. "It's...well, you already know about the bones, so I'll just come right out and tell you. We're trying to catch the culprit before the news catches wind of the whole thing and we have to delay the work on the inn."

As she took in LuAnn's words, a slow smile began to spread across Winnie's face. "I'm glad to hear it. But I have to say, I'm not sure having it by the door is going to be much help. Wasn't it the tunnel where you found the bones? Maybe you ought to put the clock in the room with the stool."

Not wanting to further insult Winnie, Janice nodded. "That's not a bad idea. If we don't get a hit from the camera in a couple of days, that's exactly what we'll do. Right, girls?"

Tess and LuAnn nodded.

"Well, you drink your tea and eat your muffins. Where do you three want the bedding you're not ready for?"

"I suppose we could stack it all on the couch in the sitting room for now." Tess looked from Janice to LuAnn. "Does that sound okay?"

With a sigh, LuAnn nodded. "That room is starting to look like we're having a rummage sale."

"It won't be long now," Janice soothed. The tea must have had its intended effect, as she was starting to relax but gaining energy at the same time. She raised her eyes to Winnie, who had returned to the counter. "You're sure lavender and peppermint are all you added to the chai?"

Without turning around, Winnie waved away her question "Oh, I might have added a couple of other herbs. Don't you worry about it."

"I'm feeling a little warm all over too," Tess said. "You'd better write out a list of ingredients if we're going to serve this. We can't go around drugging the guests."

"Well," LuAnn said, "I don't know about you two, but I think I'm going to head home for the rest of the afternoon. I'm feeling a little tired."

Tess shoved the cup back. "Yes, I don't feel much like putting away books."

"So, we're agreed," LuAnn said, following her lead and shoving back her own cup. "We'll knock off the rest of the day."

"Should we be driving after this, Winnie?"

"Oh, you'll perk right up once the fresh air hits your face."

Tess stood and grabbed onto the table to stave off the little wobble in her step. Janice wasn't sure if it was her ankle or Winnie's tea. "We have a crew of archaeologists coming tomorrow to do whatever those people do," Tess said. "Don't serve them any of this tea, or we'll find them all passed out in the tunnel."

CHAPTER TWELVE

Winnie's prediction came true and by the time Janice reached her car, her head was clearer, but she felt calmer than when she'd taken Prozac for a few months after Lawrence's death.

On the way home, she decided to make a detour to the Washington County Historical Society, which was two and a half miles from the inn. She'd gotten the photograph back from LuAnn and wanted to ask Margaret Ashworth, the local historian, if she'd ever seen it. Why she didn't think of the historical society sooner, she couldn't say. Margaret had been a good source of information for them during the last couple of months.

She drove past Robin's apartment building on the way and frowned as she saw residents standing outside on the lawn and the water utility truck parked along the street, as well as a fire truck. Poor Robin. All she needed was one more thing to go wrong in her world.

The smell of freshly cut grass greeted her as she drove past the beautifully kept riverfront park. She parked in front of the brick building that housed not only the historical society but the health department as well. Margaret greeted her as she tapped on the door and walked inside. "Janice. Lovely to see you. How are renovations coming along at the inn?"

"You know how it is. Two steps forward, one step back."

She gave the twittering laugh that Janice had grown used to over their years of acquaintance.

"What can I do for you?" she asked. "And where are your cronies? I'm not used to seeing you without them."

"They decided to knock off early. Tess's ankle is still weak and sore."

"Oh, I heard about her stepping into a hole. I know Tory Thornton felt awful."

Word got around so fast in this town. Tess wouldn't be too thrilled to know people were discussing her mishap. But at least she'd know they cared.

"It wasn't as bad as we thought it was at first. Stuart fixed her right up."

Margaret grinned. "Good to have a doctor in the family. So, what are you looking for today?"

Janice reached inside her purse, pulled out the envelope containing the photograph, and handed it to Margaret.

Margaret removed the photo from the envelope and frowned. "I've seen this exact photo."

Hope rose inside Janice as Margaret continued to study the image of the woman and child, a contemplative look on her face. "Hmm. This doesn't look like a copy."

"I'd guess it's the original." She wouldn't tell Margaret the whole story of the bones and the photo being right next to them. She would only reveal what was relevant to the information she needed. They surely didn't need this situation getting all over town.

"It's odd, though. A young woman brought in this same photo one day last week."

Janice's stomach jumped and sank at the same time. Maybe they were close to solving this part of the mystery. But what if the young woman was Robin? And where would that leave James Avery in all of this? Surely, they weren't working together. Had he been the one to tell her about the circuit box at the inn just to throw them all off the scent?

James certainly didn't give the impression that he was intelligent enough to think up a plan like that, but, as much as Janice hated to even contemplate the idea, Robin was.

"What did she want to know?"

"I imagine the same thing you do. If I'd ever seen the photo before and if I had any information about the woman and child. She said this was part of a family collection."

"So, she was an African-American woman?"

"No. She did have dark, curly hair. But she was white."

Swallowing hard, Janice met her gaze. "Did she have dimples in her cheeks?"

Margaret frowned. "I can't remember. I was looking at this."

"Okay, have you found any references to the woman and child in the journal?"

"You know I wouldn't risk damaging the pages by reading it!"

"I know you made a copy, Margaret. You wouldn't have been able to stop yourself from reading it any more than we could."

A sheepish smile raised the corners of the historian's lips. "Now that you mention it, I did make a copy. I take it you didn't find a reference in yours?"

"We haven't looked much, to be honest. There's been a lot going on at the inn." Margaret didn't need to know that Janice had kept the photo from her friends.

"Well." Margaret opened a drawer in her cluttered desk and pulled out a stack of printed papers—the journal, Janice guessed. "The closest thing I could find that might possibly be this woman was in November of 1858. But again, it's just a guess."

Just as Janice reached for the pages, her phone buzzed and Tess's name appeared on the screen. "Excuse me, Margaret. I have to take this." Janice touched the screen to accept the call. "Tess? Everything okay?"

"That depends on your definition of *okay*." Her tone was tense. Clearly, according to her definition, things were most certainly *not* okay. "Can you come back to the inn? We need to have a powwow."

A moving truck was parked outside the entrance when Janice pulled into the parking lot a few minutes later. She'd left Margaret and the journal entries, promising to look up November 1858 in her own printed copy.

Tess's son-in-law, Michael, and Isaiah were each at one end of a large buffet. Their muscles strained as they walked it up the steps, Isaiah backing up and following Michael's instructions.

"What on earth is all this? I thought you were going to pick up a sleigh bed."

"So did I," Isaiah said between grunts.

"I don't understand."

"Join the club. Miss Janice, I don't mean to be rude but..."

"Oh, of course." Janice stepped out of the way. She'd just have to get her information from her friends. She followed as the men wrestled the enormous piece of furniture into the inn and set it down in the entryway. Her jaw dropped. Several pieces of antique furniture already sat where none had when she'd left merely half an hour ago.

"He pulled up right after you left," Tess said. She sat on a red velvet settee in the middle of the room.

"What is all this? What did you and LuAnn buy on Saturday?"

"We bought a bed. That's it."

"Will you please explain? You're not making much sense."

"Apparently, when Michael got to the store, Maisie's long-time housekeeper—I wouldn't want that job, by the way—met him. Maisie died in her sleep last night. But not before writing about us in her diary. We made quite the impression, mainly due to the fact that when this place was a fancy hotel, her grandfather met her grandmother while she was working here as a maid. Remember, many of these pieces were part of the original decor."

"That explains the velvet," Janice mused.

"I imagine it's been covered over a few times, but still. Maisie's housekeeper said that, before she went to sleep, Maisie said she was just going to give us anything we wanted for the inn as it rightfully went with the place. And then she just didn't wake up, so the housekeeper wanted to honor her last wishes."

"What on earth is all of this? Tess!" LuAnn called from behind the chest of drawers Michael and Isaiah were carrying through the door.

Tess gave her the same story she'd given Janice.

LuAnn's face drained of color. "What are we going to do with it?"

Janice and Tess stared, but neither offered up a solution. Predictably, LuAnn didn't take long to offer one of her own. "We'll go through and take inventory of everything here and hire an antiques appraiser. Then we'll figure out what to do with it all." She looked to them for agreement.

"Good plan," Tess said.

Even with pulling a few of Thorn's crew from the renovations to help unload, it took over two hours to empty the truck. Some of the pieces had scuffs here and there, showing that they had clearly been used in the old home, but for the most part, they were well preserved.

"Michael," Tess said, as he set down an armoire and straightened, wiping sweat from his forehead. "Is that it?"

"There's one more thing, but it's going to take all of us to move it."

"What on earth is it, a car?"

He grinned, shaking his head. "It's a piano. A really big one."

Janice felt her heartbeat speed up. She followed him outside, and she drew a few deep breaths to calm her nerves. Surely, this couldn't be what she thought it might be.

Her legs shook in anticipation as she stepped up to the back of the truck and looked inside. Delight filled her heart as she took in the sight of a beautiful baby grand.

An hour later, the crew had all taken a much-needed iced tea break and had gone back to work. Michael had reluctantly accepted the two hundred dollars Janice insisted on giving him and gone home.

The magnificent piano sat like a work of art in the spot Janice had envisioned for the one she'd hoped to purchase for the inn. Of course, they'd need to have a piano technician come look at the instrument to see if any repair work needed to be done. Lovingly, she wiped it with a dust cloth and beamed at her friends. "God knew how much I wanted a piano."

The two friends watched her without much comment, except to say how gorgeous the instrument was. "I wonder if anyone will contest Maisie's mental abilities, giving away all these antiques," LuAnn mused.

Tess sighed and dropped into a wing chair. "According to Michael, the housekeeper seemed relieved to be rid of them.

There's no family, and Maisie's wishes were written down in her diary. I'd say as long as the housekeeper doesn't decide she wants the stuff, we're home free."

"What about taxes?" Janice sat on the bench in front of the instrument and put her fingers on the keys, unable to resist playing the first few notes of Lawrence's favorite hymn, "In the Garden." She sang the words in her head as she played the notes, imagining Lawrence's beautiful baritone filling the acoustically spectacular sanctuary of Christ Fellowship.

"We'll talk to the accountant about taxes." LuAnn crossed the floor to the piano. "This is absolutely beautiful. But, Janice..."

"Oh, I know. It's woefully out of tune. But we can get someone over here to fix that." She frowned. "Off the top of my head I can't remember who we used to tune the one at the church. I'll have to ask around."

"Janice," LuAnn said hesitantly, "did you notice the label above the keys?"

"No. But it plays beautifully. Or it will once we get it tuned. Still, it's just exquisite. Better than the one we had at the church."

"Honey, look at the name. This is a Steinway."

Janice jerked her unworthy hands away from the keys and gasped. "A Steinway?"

Tess gave a low whistle.

LuAnn ran a finger along a brass plate inside the lid. "A 1911 Steinway."

The implication was obvious. There was no way on earth Janice could justify keeping this magnificent instrument when it would likely bring them enough to stay afloat for several months.

Tess waved them both over to her chair. "I just googled what it might go for." She showed them various similar pianos for sale. Even if their piano fetched the average price, it would keep them from going broke for a couple of months.

The weight Janice had been laboring under for the last two months suddenly lessened, and the thought of surrendering another piano somehow didn't cause her as much sorrow as she'd expected it would. "Well, let's start inventorying the whole lot. Tomorrow, we'll call the appraiser, and I know a piano specialist in Columbus who I can ask to come look at the piano. Hopefully we can get this taken care of quickly."

They worked until dinnertime, then stopped for leftover soup, salad, and bread. While they ate, their conversation rolled back to the journal and photograph. Janice filled them in on the mysterious young woman who had shown Margaret the exact photograph that had been placed with the bones.

"I'd bet the Steinway that girl was Robin," Tess said. "It's no coincidence that she's working right under our noses."

LuAnn nodded. "I'm inclined to agree."

"Well, I just don't know anymore," Janice said. "Lu, are the journal pages here? Or did you take them home?"

"I put them back in the office." She rose and left the room, returning moments later with the accordion folder. "What date did Margaret give?"

November 1858

When Jason opened the door, Logan Wimber entered with his arms raised high. A sigh of relief passed through Prudence as she recognized the man holding a shotgun to the small of his back.

"Close the door, quickly," the man said. He sent Prudence an accusing glare. "We had visitors tonight at the inn. The package was delivered, I take it?"

"Thee is correct, Mr. Siloam." Mr. Siloam ran the inn and was the one person there who she had trusted with her secret.

Despite his little patience, Mr. Siloam had great compassion for those held in bondage. "Well? We have to get going. We'll tie this fellow up and put him in the cellar for a few days. If he is who he says he is, he won't mind helping out the woman."

"I told you," Logan retorted, "I'm going with her until she's safely across the border in Canada. I'm not leaving her on her own."

"The Lord will be with her, Mr. Wimber," Prudence said softly. She hated the idea of holding him there when he had been instrumental in getting Cecille off the plantation, but she could not help but see the wisdom in doing so. It would give them time to see his true motives. And even if he turned them all in, at the very least, Cecille would be free.

"Go get her." Mr. Siloam's tone rang with urgency, and his face was tense and pale.

"I am afraid she cannot be moved, Mr. Siloam. She is about to give birth."

"Can she not even be moved to the inn? It's not likely the men will be back. They've taken rooms above the saloon."

"I am afraid not. If thee will excuse me," said Prudence. "I must return to her."

LuAnn set the paper aside and stared reflectively across the room. "Isn't it fascinating to think about what this place would have looked like back then? Ladies in hoop skirts and miles of silks and lace. Elegant gentlemen in top hats escorting ladies down the steps."

Tess nodded. "And just below all of those fancy, rich travelers were secret rooms and tunnels and slaves sneaking off to the next leg on their journey to freedom."

"And our Prudence risked her life over and over again," Janice said. "She must have been so brave. I'm not sure I could have done what she did."

"There are many ways to be brave," LuAnn reassured her. "Anyone facing life all alone after three and a half decades of marriage is extremely brave. Plus, you weren't just any wife, you were a pastor's wife, on top of teaching high school and raising two children. That, my dear, is courage."

Janice smiled, appreciating her friend's attempt to raise her self-esteem. Even if she did recognize it for what it was. "So, this passage does refer to a *C*. I wonder if that woman and the baby she gave birth to that night are the ones in the photograph."

"You know what I wonder more than that?" Tess asked.

Janice and LuAnn gave her their full attention. "What?" they said in unison.

"I wonder why Robin put those bones in our tunnel. I think we ought to come right out and ask her."

"We don't know that she did it for sure," Janice said.

"Who else?" Tess shot back.

LuAnn nodded. "She has a point, Janice. There's an awful lot of coincidence."

"Well, I think we should give her the benefit of the doubt." Janice frowned as something from the journal niggled at her. Something familiar she hadn't been able to put her finger on. "Did she call one of the men Wimber? Lu, can I see the journal?"

LuAnn slid the pages across the table to her.

"Look! The white man Prudence was with. His first name was L. But she used his last name: Wimber."

"So?" Tess said.

"Tess! Wimber. *The* Wimbers?"

"Oh! Those Wimbers."

A huff came from LuAnn. "Could you please not say 'Wimbers' again if you aren't going to expound?"

Janice laughed. "I'm sorry. Isaiah Wimber works on our crew."

"The guy Janice hopes will marry Stacy."

"I'm not going to lie," Janice admitted. "He's a good catch. Mostly because he's a good, solid, Christian man."

"Okay, so he has the same last name as this L. Wimber from the journal."

"Right." Janice's pulse raced in her veins as she started to see a connection. Nothing she could put her finger on, but enough of a coincidence that there just *had* to be a story.

"Right what?"

"What I'm trying to say, is that there is a family named Wimber still to this day in Williamstown, West Virginia. I'm guessing the slave woman that Prudence rowed over from the Virginia—which it still would have been in 1858, before secession—side of the river that night was running from the Wimber plantation."

"Stuart's archaeologist is coming tomorrow," LuAnn said. "Maybe she and her team will be able to find something. I asked Winnie to make some muffins or tarts or some sort of refreshments for them."

Tess sighed. "That'll make them stay longer."

"Be that as it may," LuAnn said, "it's the polite thing to do."

"I suppose."

"Hello!" someone called from the front door. "Ladies!" The tone had grown alarmed.

"Sounds like Margaret Ashworth," LuAnn said. "I'd better go in there before she gets lost in that maze of furniture."

She returned a couple of minutes later, escorting Margaret.

"Those are such exquisite pieces in there," Margaret said. "Goodness gracious, what I wouldn't give to have those in my home."

"We'll be putting a lot of it up for sale," Tess said, "so feel free to bid."

"Oh, like I could ever afford those." Margaret laughed. "Anyway, I'm glad I saw your cars. We never finished our conversation about the photograph you brought in today, Janice."

"Thank you for thinking of us," Janice replied.

"Oh dear, it wasn't a secret that you were asking about the photo, was it?"

"Of course not," Tess said. "We tell each other everything."

Janice smiled at her friend, especially in light of the fact that she'd withheld the photograph from them in the first place.

Margaret's expression dropped a little in disappointment. Janice couldn't imagine thriving off of drama like that. "I'm so glad to hear it. So you'll want to see this too." She spread a map over the table. "The girl who came into my office with that photo also asked about a local map from the mid- to late-1800s. So much was destroyed during the fire of 1859, so this was likely drawn up after that."

"Or it just survived."

Margaret shrugged. "Maybe."

Janice walked around the table so she didn't have to look at the map upside down. "Did she say why she was interested in the map?"

"She did."

The three ladies of the inn perked up, waiting, while Margaret stared silently at the map. They knew she liked nothing more than to draw out her information with dramatics, and clearly, she was enjoying keeping them in suspense.

"Well?" Tess said, apparently coming to the end of her patience.

"Well, I don't know if I should say. I do have to keep some things confidential."

"Then why did you bring it over in the first place, Margaret?" LuAnn said, her tone forcibly amiable.

"All right. I'll be honest with you, since we're all friends. I saw Michael picking up some barbeque for dinner—he said Lizzie isn't feeling well, Tess. Anyway, he mentioned he'd been moving antiques for you all afternoon, and I was just dying to get a look. I hope you don't mind me coming over under false pretenses."

"Why would we?" LuAnn smiled. "Like you said, we're all friends. Would you care for some tea? Winnie made the most wonderful blend earlier."

Margaret's face lit up at the invitation. "That would be lovely. Thank you."

It occurred to Janice that Margaret didn't have many real friends. Not that she couldn't find people to get along with, but maybe if she had a friend, she'd be nicer.

LuAnn set the kettle on the stove. "Can you just believe all those beautiful antique pieces in there?" she said. LuAnn was a master at drawing people into conversation. Surely, she had a plan for getting Margaret to open up about the map.

"You might want to roll that up, Margaret," Tess said, grudgingly. "Wouldn't want to spill anything on it."

"Oh, yes, I probably should."

Disappointment wound through Janice. Why on earth would Margaret have brought the map over in the first place if she had no intention of telling them what the woman was after? And now she seemed more interested in talking about the furniture in the other room.

"To answer your question, LuAnn," she said, "the pieces are so perfectly preserved, it's unbelievable. When I walked through the maze of antiques out there, I recognized a bathroom vanity that, unless I'm mistaken, is early twentieth century. I'd just love something like that in my formal restroom. It's just the thing I've been looking for."

Was it Janice's imagination, or was Margaret actually offering to trade information for an antique worth who knew how much?

"You mean the marble-topped one?" Tess asked.

"Oh, is that marble?" Summoning all her innocence, Margaret ran her french manicured nail along the rolled-up map.

"Pretty sure it is." Tess glanced at Janice in exasperation.

"Drink your tea, dear," LuAnn said, as she set the cup in front of Margaret.

"Oh, aren't the rest of you having any?"

"We all still have iced tea from dinner."

Janice sent an anxious glance toward Margaret's teacup as she let it sit there.

"This smells heavenly. So, do tell me how all those antiques came to be yours." She gave a short laugh. "Michael wouldn't tell me a thing, and I know you couldn't possibly have purchased all of that on your retirement and your husbands' life insurance."

Had she actually just said life insurance? Janice couldn't decide if Margaret was more socially awkward or just mean.

"What do you think of the tea?" Tess asked.

Margaret blew into the cup, then lifted it to her lips. "Well, it's rather lovely, isn't it? What is it?"

"Lavender and peppermint in chai."

By unspoken consent, none of them mentioned the special herbs that only Winnie and God knew she'd put into that blend.

"It has an odd little kick to it, doesn't it?" she said after the third or fourth sip.

"That's the chai," Tess said. "Now, the woman who came in with the photograph, what was it she wanted to know?"

A sly smile touched Margaret's lips. "Well, first you all were going to tell me about that vanity in there—marble, you said?"

Clearly, she hadn't taken in enough of the tea yet. LuAnn launched into the tale of how they met the woman who owned all of those things. By the time she was finished, Margaret was down to half a cup and suppressing one yawn after another.

"Nothing wonderful like that ever happens to me," she complained.

"You mean like someone dying?"

"Exactly." She sighed loudly. "No one ever gives me anything." She lifted her shoulders. "Oh, well. I suppose that's why God gave me two capable hands. I just have to work and save for what I want."

"Implying what, exactly?" The challenge in Tess's voice was unmistakable. "You think we took advantage of a senile old woman?"

Goodness gracious goat. Tess was going to ruin the whole thing if she didn't lower her hackles.

Janice would've given her a good kick in the leg, but she was on her bad ankle side. Instead, she raised her eyebrow at her friend. "I think what Margaret meant was that we were very blessed to fall into an elderly woman's good graces that way."

Margaret frowned. "I guess that's what I meant."

"How are things at the historical society these days?" LuAnn asked. "We are so blessed to have someone with your impeccable knowledge of the area. That must be why everyone comes to you when they need help with a location that isn't marked on contemporary maps. Like that woman who came in with the photograph. What was it you said she was looking for?"

Margaret gave a slight wave of her hand. "Oh, well, I'd never seen her before. But she said she had ancestors from this area, and she wanted to know how to find their graves." She gave another sly smile that included all three. "I might even be inclined to show you the exact area she snapped with her phone camera—if we can talk some more about that vanity."

Figures, Janice thought. Rather than dull her senses and make her more agreeable, the tea had served to sharpen Margaret's powers of negotiation. Janice supposed that served them right. God was probably having a good laugh at their expense.

CHAPTER THIRTEEN

All in all, it was worth selling Margaret the vanity for half its value to get the information she had. Although technically, it was extortion.

"She should be arrested for what she did," Tess said, fuming, as she glanced at the map. "No scruples."

"Well, at least she gave us the map and marked off the places the woman was most interested in." Janice would've given her the vanity for free for access to the map. But Tess wouldn't hear of it.

Tess snorted. "You know she made this copy because she intended to scope out the goods and force us into a trade."

"Well, in all fairness, we did get those things for free," LuAnn said.

Tess glared in return.

LuAnn waved to get her friends' attention. "All right," she said. "Let's run down what we have so far." Her notebook was open in front of her, and she tapped the table with her pen. "Thursday, Janice found the bones."

"And the photo," Janice reminded Tess and LuAnn. "I'm just still so sorry for keeping that from you two."

"It's over," Tess said, her huffy attitude gone as she patted Janice's hand.

LuAnn nodded without looking up from her notebook as she made out their timeline. "Yes, and we love and forgive you, so let's move on. Janice found the bones and the photo on Thursday."

"The same day you saw James Avery coming through the tunnel exit by the river," Tess said.

"He's still my prime suspect," Janice said, emphatically.

"We know." Tess nodded and adjusted her foot, which was propped on the chair next to where she sat. "And I still think Robin is involved."

Janice sighed. "We know."

"We need to talk about another suspect..." LuAnn said hesitantly.

"If you mean the *person of interest*," Janice said, unable to keep her tone light, "I thought we'd pretty much eliminated my son considering the fact that James brought in the mud."

LuAnn drew in a breath and spoke softly. "Well, there's still the fact that James mentioned seeing Stuart here at the inn after dark. I admit he's the least likely on the list, but we can't completely eliminate him."

"Fine," Janice said tersely, trying not to take it personally that her friends—who had watched him grow up—suspected her son of something nefarious. "Let's keep going. Friday, James didn't come to work again, and we caught him handing something off to a man we've never seen before."

Tess nodded. "Then we nearly died—thanks to your dark glasses, Lu—following him and lost him."

LuAnn wrote as they talked, then she looked up. "We forgot to mention that morning we went to Robin's apartment, but she doesn't have a dog like she claimed. Then we paid the electric bill."

"Then Brad bought us lunch," Tess reminded the group.

The change of subject soothed Janice's ruffled feathers, and she couldn't help but smile at what Tess wasn't saying about Brad.

"Right." LuAnn kept writing, keeping her gaze on the notebook. "On Saturday, we went shopping, so no new suspects."

Tess adjusted her leg again. "But we met a woman who felt that we were a divine connection and gave us her family heirlooms and mysteriously died the next day."

"Yes," Janice said. "Even against the biggest odds, we were able to buy the building and we've already overcome so many obstacles."

LuAnn's eyes were bright with unshed tears. "My greatest desire in life is to have a place for ministry, you both know that. I want the inn to be a place people come to feel refreshed and loved. The antiques will mean we don't have to buy as much furniture, but also the pieces we sell will help us start off, if not in the black, then almost to the line."

Janice felt her eyes well up, and she could see that Tess was choking up too. They knew LuAnn's dream had always been to teach until retirement and then freefall into God's ultimate purpose for her. It did seem like God had orchestrated the meeting with Maisie, who had a familial connection to the inn.

Blinking away the tears, LuAnn brought her attention back to the notebook. "Okay, Sunday, James accused our Stuey of sneaking into the inn at night. But in light of the fact that James was the one I saw coming out of the tunnel, and that Robin is presumably the dark-haired woman who talked to Margaret, both of them seem more likely to be guilty. I say we table the idea of Stu's involvement until we watch the video from the basement and have a chance to confront him."

"I concur," Tess said with an emphatic nod.

LuAnn's use of Stuart's childhood nickname brought a smile to Janice's lips and lightened the heaviness that had settled on her heart at the very idea that her friends suspected her son.

LuAnn added a question mark next to Stuart's name on the list then looked up. "And speaking of the dark-haired woman, the map is the last thing we need to add to the list. It has to be an important piece of the puzzle."

"And we still have no idea what Robin's nonexistent dog has to do with any of this."

A loud ring made them all about jump out of their skins. "What on earth?" Tess said, her palm pressed against her chest.

Janice rose and went to the counter just as the ringing sounded again. "Phone." They'd had the phone installed at the inn for business calls, but this was the first time it had rung.

"Answer with the inn name," LuAnn reminded her.

"Wayfarers Inn, this is Janice speaking." Janice grinned as Tess and Lu each gave her a thumbs-up.

"Mrs. Eastman? This is Chief Mayfield. We just wanted to let you ladies know we've arrested James Avery."

"I knew he was the one who planted those bones!"

He hesitated. "I don't know about that. But he's apparently been using the tunnels over there to hide stolen copper wire since before y'all bought the building."

"Copper wire?"

"What copper wire?" LuAnn asked. "Who is that?"

Janice placed her hand over the receiver. "James was arrested for stealing copper wire," she whispered. "He's been using the tunnels to hide his loot."

Tess frowned. "What about the bones?"

Janice moved her hand. "Chief Mayfield, what did you find out about the bones?"

"Ma'am, we still don't know anything about who did that. Mr. Avery only confessed to stealing and hiding his contraband at your inn."

With a sigh, Janice resigned herself to not solving that particular mystery tonight. "Well, thanks for letting us know."

"Wait, one more thing, Mrs. Eastman."

"Yes?"

"I'm sorry, but your inn is a crime scene. Based on the new information we've obtained, we'll have to search the tunnel again."

Janice groaned. "Not again!" Last month, it had been the FBI declaring the inn a crime scene.

"What?" LuAnn asked.

"When do you plan to be here? We were just about to leave for the night."

"I'm afraid we're already on our way. We won't stay any longer than necessary."

She thanked him and hung up. "Looks like we're in for a late one." She sighed. "Who's up for another night in a lovely old inn?"

Janice smiled as she heard the sound of Larry's childish voice calling out to her through the cluttered entrance. When she'd phoned to let Stacy know she would be staying at the inn and why, she'd been pleasantly surprised by her daughter's offer to bring her a change of clothing and other essentials from home.

"Nana!" Larry called again.

She laughed and greeted them at the sitting room doorway. "I'm here."

Stacy looked around in wonder at the furniture. She caressed a sleek wooden armoire. "What is all this? These pieces are fantastic." She turned to Janice with a look of concern as she dropped her tone. "Did Aunt Lu get spend happy?"

"God provided all of this for free, Stace." She offered the *Reader's Digest* condensed version of the events leading to the antiques coming into their possession. "Just come and look at this." She waved her into the living room and walked her straight to the piano.

Stacy's jaw dropped. "Oh, Mama. This is stunning."

"It's a Steinway," Janice said, finding she couldn't speak above a whisper as she breathed out the name.

Stacy's eyes widened. "What? Mother, are you kidding me? That lady gave you a *Steinway* for *free?*"

"The Lord provided for us." Janice swallowed hard. "The proceeds will keep us financially secure as we open the inn, so our families can stop worrying we're in over our heads."

"I mean, that's good, I guess. But wow, too bad you can't keep this." The look of disappointment on her face reminded Janice of the Christmas Stacy had asked for a video game system, but the best they could do for their daughter was a much less expensive handheld game. She'd recovered valiantly, but the initial disappointment had broken Janice's heart.

Stacy slung an arm around her and squeezed. "I'm so sorry, Mom. I wish you could keep it. But of course, an instrument like this will bring in a ton of money. And honestly, I know it will make Stu and me both feel a lot better." She smiled. "Can you play Daddy's song on it? I mean, while it's here, you might as well tickle the ol' ivories."

Despite her feelings of intimidation over sitting at the piano of pianos, there was no way Janice was going to deny her daughter's request. She sat down, placed her fingers on the keys, and played "In the Garden" again. She sang and as she did, Stacy joined in with her beautiful alto. Even Larry joined in on the chorus with pitch not-so-perfect high tones of a child, scooting onto the bench next to Janice.

She and Stacy both wiped away tears when they sang the last line, "And the joy we share as we tarry there, none other has ever known."

"I haven't sung a hymn in ages," Stacy said. "But I could almost hear Dad singing along, couldn't you?"

Emotion rendered Janice unable to answer without dissolving into tears, so she simply nodded. She felt more than Lawrence in the room; she felt the presence of God. He was clearly drawing Stacy back to Him. Perhaps the Steinway didn't belong to Janice, but God had given her the gift of hope for her daughter through it, and she couldn't help but inwardly praise Him for these past few moments.

"Mom," Stacy said tentatively, "do you think it would be okay for me to see the second-floor rooms? Lizzie told me they're just darling, and I've been waiting for you to show me. If you want to, that is."

Janice let out a gasp. "Sweetheart, you haven't seen them yet? No, of course you haven't. Not since they were finished and all put together. I'm so scatterbrained sometimes."

Janice couldn't remember enjoying anything as much, lately, as taking her daughter and grandson on a tour of the beautifully decorated rooms. Stacy stood in the middle of the honeymoon suite and shook her head. "It's fantastic. You must be so excited."

Excited was one word to describe how she felt right now. But even more than that, she was completely confused by the sudden change in Stacy's attitude.

"I hear you're going to meet Avi tomorrow," Stacy said. "Stu said she's bringing her graduate students to look for some bone fragments."

"That's right. How serious do you think he is about this woman?"

Stacy shrugged. "Who knows? Three months is pretty much his record, so it'll be interesting to see if he gets cold feet."

Janice nodded and plopped onto one of the chairs. "What do you think it is about her that's different from the other women he's dated over the years?"

Following her lead, Stacy took the chair on the other side of a beautiful round table they'd restored after discovering it in the basement. "I'm not sure. I mean, she's pretty but not drop-dead gorgeous. She's sort of a science nerd, so I guess they have that in common." She frowned. "I know Stu has said he wants a woman who has a strong sense of her own identity."

"What does that even mean?"

Stacy shrugged again. "I guess that he wants someone with her own goals and own sense of who she is, with or without him. In other words, he doesn't want a woman who changes to suit his personality and job."

Stung, Janice considered her words for a few seconds before replying. "So, what you're saying is he doesn't want someone like his mother?"

Stacy grinned and shook her head. "I think he wants someone exactly like his mother. You were the Proverbs 31 woman, Mom. You had a career you loved, took great care of your family, had good friends, and still somehow found the energy to help Daddy in his ministry. You know he couldn't have done half what he did without you behind him. But part of that meant you had to know who you were inside. Otherwise, you'd have crumbled under all the stress."

The woman Stacy described seemed like a stranger to Janice. Was that the way her daughter truly saw her?

"You've been a tough act to follow, Mom. And now you're opening an inn that's going to be the talk of the town. Sometimes, I actually get jealous"—she gave a nervous laugh—"of my own mother for outshining me."

Was this the source of her daughter's snide remarks lately? "What do you mean?"

"Ma, come on." She cast a cautious glance at Larry. "Let's just say I haven't accomplished one third of the things at thirty-two years old that you did by the time you were twenty-five." She drew in a deep breath and exhaled. "I've been thinking of going back to school. Not medical school but something that would help me take better care of Larry's needs and, quite frankly, make me happier with myself. Is that crazy at my age?"

The impressive of thirty-two? Janice refrained from rolling her eyes. "Of course it's not crazy. You don't have to be a doctor to find something you love doing. With all the hours you have already, it would only be a matter of entering a degree program and taking a year or two of upper-level courses."

Hope rose in Stacy's eyes. "I think I might enjoy teaching. It's something I've considered." A shadow passed over her face. "I'm not sure how I can afford it, though. And it will be time-consuming going to classes and working."

"I'll help. Once my suite is finished, I can set up a place for Larry to play and even sleep over if you need him to stay with me on occasion."

"They do have online courses that I could probably take. I'll have to look into financial stuff. But I'm sure I can work that out."

Stacy had exhausted her meager college fund by the time she graduated with her Bachelor of Science degree, but Janice was pretty sure she could help some. "God will make a way, Stacy. If all those antiques down there aren't proof of that, I don't know what is." She took a deep breath. "I'm glad you've told me what's been bothering you lately. I was afraid you were upset that the inn was taking all my time."

Stacy tilted her head and smiled at her. "Mom. I'm not a kid anymore. I understand how much effort you and Aunt Lu and Aunt Tess are putting into this." She stood and came around the table, bent down, and gave Janice a big hug. "I'm so proud of you, and I can't wait for opening day. Larry and I know you love us and are always there for us anytime we need you."

LuAnn and Tess were waiting when they descended the stairs a few minutes later, arm in arm. "Hey, Stace. What do you think?" Tess asked.

"It's incredible. You three are going to make a killing."

"From your lips to God's ears," LuAnn said, hugging her. She turned her attention to Larry, running her hand over his curls. "Are you staying out of trouble, little man?"

"Not all the time."

They laughed, and Janice felt lighter than she had in a year.

With a promise to get online and start looking for teaching programs, Stacy took Larry home so she could put him to bed. The three friends adjourned to the living room to wait until the police were finished searching the tunnel.

Officer Randy Lewis found them forty-five minutes later. He carried two large boxes and his partner carried two more. "The wire was just where he said it was." He gave them a weary smile. "I'm sorry we had to come over so late. But the chief wanted me to let you know, it was your tip that helped us catch him. The last few months, James has been slowly moving the wire from the tunnel. So, this is the last of it."

"But how?" LuAnn asked. "We've been down in that tunnel several times and haven't seen a thing."

"Inside the walls, there's a hiding place you probably just haven't come across yet. It's not obvious to the naked eye. We only found it because Avery told us exactly where to look."

"Did you leave it accessible?" LuAnn asked, her eyes shining with excitement.

Janice shuddered at the very thought of going into yet another dark room. LuAnn could have that adventure all she wanted.

Randy grinned. "Yes, ma'am. We left the stone front leaning against the wall. There was a wooden door behind it that led into a room not much bigger than a closet. My guess is that it was there to hide no more than two or three runaways if the tunnel was discovered while they were trying to get away."

LuAnn, still fascinated with the thought of yet another revealed secret about the history of the inn, addressed Randy. "How did he know where the room was located in the first place?"

Randy shook his head. "I don't know, ma'am."

"How on earth did you get James to tell you where his hiding place was?" Tess asked.

Janice almost felt sorry for Randy having so many questions fired at him all at once. But to his credit, he remained polite and accommodating. "Turns out some of the fingerprints on the shovel belonged to Avery's son. He'd gotten in some trouble a few years back and his prints were in our database. When we went to question him, he told us his dad had borrowed the shovel a while ago. So, we decided to go by Avery's." He grinned. "He thought we were there to arrest him about the wire and confessed."

"And you don't think James's son was involved at all?"

"No, ma'am. It doesn't seem so."

They walked Randy and his partner out into the warm, dark night. By the time they went inside and locked the doors, it was after ten, and Janice could barely keep her eyes open.

The next day would be busy. They had to call an antiques appraiser and hope for a quick appointment. Stuart's new girlfriend would be here then as well.

Janice fell into bed a few minutes later, bone weary but heart happy. Some days felt empty and hard to walk through, but not this day. As she floated to sleep on the soft new mattress, she breathed a prayer of thanks.

November 1858

Cecille gave birth to a fat, squalling baby girl within an hour of Siloam's visit to the house. The woman fell into an exhausted sleep minutes after Prudence tucked the baby into the crook of her arm and didn't budge when the baby woke up fussing.

Willa quieted the minute Prudence snuggled her close. Smiling down at the precious little one who stared up at her with dark eyes, Prudence prayed that she and her mother would find their way to their promised land. She shivered as she grew still and realized just how chilled the room was. Stepping into the living room, she immediately felt its warmth and walked to the wooden rocking chair.

Jason had made them a pallet close to the fire, but he still sat at the table, staring out the front window as if expecting a mob to descend upon them at any moment.

"Mr. Siloam went back to the inn?" Prudence asked, lowering herself carefully into the chair.

Jason gave a curt nod. "He said to tell thee he will return tomorrow night and the woman must be ready to go or he cannot guarantee safe passage for another two weeks."

"How does he expect a woman who has just given birth to be able to travel so quickly?"

Jason shook his head and rose and crossed the room to her. "I know not. But dear one, thee knows that she cannot remain here. Spending even a day in this house, she brings us too much danger. If we could move her to the cellar..."

"No." Prudence shook her head and stared down at baby Willa. "She must not be moved a minute sooner than necessary. Husband, the steps into the basement would be much too hard for her to climb down."

He expelled a heavy breath. "I reckon thee is right. Forgive my lack of faith. I cannot bear the thought of thee in such danger."

Prudence reached up one hand and pressed it to his scratchy face. "But look, my love. Look at what God has given us to do. Imagine. This beautiful little girl will never know the chains of bondage. She'll be free to grow into the woman God created her to be. She'll fall in love and marry and have children of her own. Almighty God never promised that we would not suffer for His cause. Quite the opposite, in fact."

His eyes softened as he knelt beside the chair and studied the beautiful infant. "Will she remain white?"

Prudence nodded. "It is very likely. Her mother is rather light skinned, and from what I gather, her father is Logan's brother. He impregnated Cecille purposely to give his wife another child after his first child with Cecille easily passed for white."

Drawing a deep breath, Jason reached for Willa. "May I?"

"Of course."

He walked closer to the fire, bouncing the baby gently. Prudence rose and followed him, laying her head on his shoulder. "Dear, I must tell thee something I have been keeping from you."

Jason turned sharply to her and met her gaze. "What is it?" he asked with caution.

Joy bubbled inside of her. "I am with child again."

His eyes grew big, and slowly it dawned what she had confided. "And thee are sure?"

She nodded. "I believe our child will be born in early summer."

"Hast thee seen the midwife?"

"Soon."

"This visitor must be the last one until after our child is born, if the Lord wills we keep him."

Prudence had known he would insist. And she would obey.

"I must keep my position at the inn, and I will help after they come to the inn, but I will not deliver any more packages that involve me having to row the boat." She did not want to hurt his pride, but he was not as able to work as he once was, and the wages she contributed to their household would come in handy with a new baby coming.

There was still hesitation in his eyes, but he nodded agreement.

A loud knock shook the door, and it flew open. Mr. Siloam strode inside. He had brought his wagon and it was clear he didn't intend to wait twenty-four hours to move Cecille.

"I was delivering a message at the saloon tonight. The men who came to the inn earlier were loud and drunk and talking about the package. And we can apparently trust that Logan Wimber is helping the woman, because there's a reward on his head—dead or alive—of one thousand dollars. And that much more for the woman. I overheard them say they intend to search every home, barn, and outhouse along the Muskingum River until they find them."

Prudence gasped. "Mr. Siloam, she has just given birth to this babe. We cannot move her or she will die."

"And if we do not move her now, young woman, many more people will either die or be arrested. If we do not move her now, we may never have another opportunity to lead another precious soul to safety."

The door to the bedroom opened and a shaky Cecille appeared. "I'll be fine, ma'am. Thank you for all you've done."

Prudence took Willa from Jason. "Husband, please go and free Mr. Wimber so he may accompany Cecille as is his wish."

Jason frowned, turning to Mr. Siloam. "And thee are convinced he is no threat to us?"

"As convinced as I can be. I'm putting myself and our whole company at risk, as well as you and your wife, if I am wrong. But the reward on his head makes it too dangerous for you to keep him here as we originally planned."

While Prudence packed a bag with two of her spare dresses and a fresh nightgown for Cecille, and insisted she take the garments, Mr. Siloam made a pallet in the back of his wagon with heavy quilts he'd brought from the inn. By the time Cecille was ready, Jason had entered the living room with Logan.

Lifting Cecille gently into his arms, Logan carried her to the wagon. Prudence grabbed her coat and slid it on, but Jason took her arm gently to detain her. "Pru. We had an agreement."

"Dear, I must see this through. Cecille has just given birth. She will need a woman to care for her."

"She's right," Mr. Siloam said. "We won't be able to move her on to the next station tomorrow night. Not unless Rafe Wimber and his posse leave the area. But I don't think he will until he gets the sheriff involved and pays the man to go house to house searching."

Jason did not argue further. Instead her pulled her close and held tightly. She felt him press a kiss to her head before he released her. "Go with God, my dear."

CHAPTER FOURTEEN

No one else was stirring in the inn when Janice slipped into her robe, pulled on her slippers, and walked down the stairs before dawn the next morning. The inn felt strange and echoey in the stillness. No activity from the crew, the kitchen dark except for a nightlight plugged in above the countertop, and no coffee made. Janice switched on the light and headed for the coffeepot.

When the coffee finished brewing, she carried a large mug onto the porch and sat in one of the wicker chairs as the world awakened.

She closed her eyes as the quiet shrouded her in peace. *Good morning, Father. You outdid yourself in goodness yesterday. I don't know how to thank You.* In moments like this, it was so easy to feel loved and at peace.

She sipped her coffee and breathed in deeply the humid river air. Some tourists didn't enjoy the smell of the river, but Janice did. It reminded her of summer swimming, fishing with her father, paddleboat trips down the river on calm, lazy days. Winter had its memories too, but the river came alive during the warmth of summer.

Her peaceful reminiscing was shattered as high-pitched, incessant barking reached her ears. Annoyed, she scanned the area, trying to find the source. A car door opened in the parking lot, and she frowned as she recognized Robin in the glow from the streetlights. Janice stood and walked to the edge of the porch.

"Robin?" she called softly. She took in a sharp breath. The woman was walking a dog. A tiny, white, hairy mutt whose stump of a tail was moving back and forth crazily as she approached.

"Mrs. Eastman," Robin said, hesitantly. "You're up early."

"I could say the same about you. What on earth are you doing here at five in the morning?"

She hesitated before answering. "Walking my dog?"

Janice frowned in confusion. "I'm not sure I understand. You drove two miles to the inn just to walk your dog?" She almost asked where the dog had been on Friday when they went to Robin's apartment but bit her tongue in time. But boy, was Tess going to feel awful when she discovered the truth.

Robin drew in a breath, then exhaled. "A pipe burst in my apartment yesterday. Throughout the whole building actually. I...slept in my car."

Janice's mind went to the day before when she'd driven past all the hoopla outside of Robin's building. "You...slept in your *car*?" *Lord, were You trying to speak to me when I drove by her building yesterday?*

"Yes. But it's not as bad as it sounds." She offered her beautiful smile. "I've slept in my car plenty of times."

Somehow, that didn't help one bit. "Well," Janice said, "I'm about to go start breakfast. You finish with the dog and come inside. You can shower upstairs and then have breakfast with us." She cast a cautious glance at the dog. "He's potty trained?"

Robin smiled again. "Yes, she's housebroken. But, you don't have to..."

"Now, no argument. I insist you join us for breakfast."

Janice couldn't be sure in the dim predawn light, but she was almost sure she saw a glassy sheen in Robin's eyes.

"Thank you." She turned to the dog. "Come on, Cecille, let's go for our walk."

When Robin returned to the inn, Janice escorted her upstairs to the Lily and Lace room, on the second floor, where she'd slept the night before. The dog seemed to take a shine to her and followed her downstairs to the kitchen while Robin showered and dressed for the day. "Well, Cecille," she said as she pulled strawberry muffins from the oven and scrambled some eggs, "I guess you weren't a lie of convenience after all."

The thought delighted Janice. She still believed more would be revealed about the bones through James's arrest. He himself had told them there were other uses for the inn besides an inn. Had he meant to store his stolen items? It seemed possible that the bones were either a way to scare them off of the project or simply a way to sabotage their efforts while he removed his loot. Either way, her vote for the guilty party was still James Avery.

Bleary-eyed, Tess and LuAnn entered the kitchen just as Janice placed four plates on the table. "Morning, ladies," Janice said cheerily.

Tess limped to the table and took a seat, and then she noticed the tiny dog lying in the corner. "Where did that come from?"

Janice grinned, setting the bowl of eggs on the table. "That's Cecille. Robin's dog."

LuAnn poured coffee for herself and Tess and cast a wary glance at the dog. Cecille raised her head as though she knew she was the star of the show and thumped her stumpy tail. "What on earth?"

"Robin's upstairs taking a shower." While Janice placed muffins in a basket, fresh strawberries in a bowl, and bacon on a platter, she told them about Robin's apartment.

"She slept in her car?" Tess's face was filled with sympathy and indignation. "Surely she saw our lights on. Why didn't she just come inside? The honeymoon suite has two rooms. She could've slept on the fold-out bed."

"Are we allowing guests to bring pets?" LuAnn asked, helping to set the food on the table. "I think it's something we need to discuss. Not that we wouldn't have allowed Robin to bring that darling little pup." She smiled at Cecille. "Hey, sweetheart. You're such a pretty little girl."

Cecille hopped up, and her little body practically quivered with excitement at the attention. LuAnn laughed with delight. She pulled Cecille into her arms and received a lick on her cheek as a reward.

Tess wrinkled her nose at the display. "That's disgusting, Lu. Put it down and go wash your hands and face." She gave a grudging smile at the way the dog settled against LuAnn's shoulder. "So, Robin has a dog after all. I still say..."

Janice shook her head and pressed her finger to her lips. "She could come in any second." They would have to table the discussion about Robin and the dog.

A moment later, Robin entered the kitchen, her springy hair wet and pulled up into a clip. She smiled with her entire face when she saw Cecille in LuAnn's arms. "Looks like she made a new friend."

"Or I did." LuAnn chuckled and set Cecille down on the floor.

Janice knew all three of them were dying to learn where that dog and any sign of a dog had been on Friday. But, of course, they couldn't very well come right out and ask.

The dog camped out under the table at LuAnn's feet as they ate their breakfast. At Janice's insistence, Robin dove into the food. "This is such a treat. I hardly ever have more than a protein bar and coffee in the morning."

"That's not good," Tess said, clearly warming up to Robin. "As hard as you work, you should be eating three square meals every day. You don't want to get run down."

"Well, you saw how much I ate at lunch yesterday—and thank you again, by the way. I'm usually starving by ten, so by the time lunch rolls around, I eat like a trucker."

From the corner of her eye, Janice saw LuAnn break off a bite of bacon and slyly feed it to Cecille.

"What do you do with Cecille while you're at work?" Tess said. Janice couldn't help but wonder if she still suspected Robin, or if Tess was as confused as she was that no trace of Cecille had been evident in her apartment.

Robin washed down a bite of food with a swig of her coffee. "Usually, she stays at home. I hate leaving her all day, but my neighbor checks in on her, and sometimes she just stays with him if he's not planning to go anywhere." She smiled. "He's a blogger and tests video games for a living, which is why he can't afford a better apartment." She laughed.

So, it was possible Cecille had been at the young man's apartment Friday. Well, there was just no good way to ask.

"What do you intend to do with her while you're working today?" Tess asked.

"I was hoping you might let me tie her up on the porch? I'll check on her as much as I can."

LuAnn frowned, this time unabashedly giving the dog the rest of her bacon. "Do you tie her up often?"

"Never. I'm not sure how she'll respond. But I can't leave her in the car, even with the window cracked. By midmorning, it's too hot."

"Well, of course you can't leave the poor thing in the car. Do you know how hot it gets inside a vehicle when it's eighty-five degrees outside?" LuAnn reached down and gathered Cecille onto her lap. "They say it reaches at least another twenty degrees, maybe even more. And she can't stay tied up, either. She would be terrified."

Tess cast a knowing look to Janice. "What do you suggest, Lu?"

"Well, I suppose she can be my little companion today. Do you have her food and water dishes in the car, Robin?"

Robin's eyes softened. "I'll go get them as soon as I help clean up."

"Don't even think about that," Janice said. "You have to get to work in a little while. And there's no point in protesting, because we insist."

Robin glanced around the table at the three of them and shrugged her concession. "Okay, then." She nodded. "I'll just take Cecille for a walk and bring her dishes in when she's done. Thank you so much for breakfast. It was a real treat for me. And Ms. Sherrill," she said, "I can't thank you enough for watching Cecille."

"We'll get along just fine."

Janice gathered in a deep breath and reached for the clock they'd set on a storage shelf above the washer and dryer. It gave them the best view of the door to the loading area. Janice felt around for the tiny memory card. When Stacy had used the camera so she could see Larry throughout the workday, she'd signed into a website, but Janice didn't have the login information, and asking would only encourage questions from Stacy. She didn't want to have to admit to her daughter that they were spying just in case Stuart, for some reason, really was sneaking into the inn.

Frowning, Janice turned the clock over, then her heart began to beat in double time. The memory card wasn't there. She knew it had been the day before because she'd checked it specifically before pressing the camera's power button. Someone must have removed it between the time she had set the camera up and now. That was the only explanation.

Had one of her friends decided to spare her the heartbreak of seeing her own son tiptoeing through the basement doing only the Lord knew what? She set the clock back on the shelf and hurried upstairs, hanging onto the railing to avoid a slip.

When she reached the kitchen, Winnie had set out some of the pastries she'd made and frozen over the past week. She had baked them as refreshments for the archaeological team coming in a little while.

Tess, LuAnn, and Winnie all sat, lingering over coffee. Janice took them all in with a sweeping glance. "Did any of you take the memory card out of the clock?"

The three women at the table looked from one to the other, then to Janice. "Are you sure you remembered to put it in there?" Tess asked.

"You know I did. You were sitting right there!"

Winnie shrugged. "Someone must've got to it before you, then."

"But who would even know it was there except us?" Suspicion narrowed Janice's gaze. "Did you do it, Winnie?"

The shrewd woman cast a sharp glance at her. "Now, what good reason could I have to care one way or another about that camera being down there?"

"Well, you did think we were spying on you." Tess set her cup on the table.

Winnie stared at her. "I'm not dignifying that with an answer."

"Well, I guess we have another mystery on our hands. Someone around here figured out about the camera and took the card before we could catch them red-handed. Did one of you tell the workers it was there?"

"Of course not," LuAnn said. "Janice, are you sure you didn't tell Robin? Or give Stuart a heads-up?"

Insulted to her core, Janice lifted her chin. "My answer is the same as Winnie's. I'm not dignifying that with an answer."

Winnie gave her a nod of approval. "That's what I'm talking about."

"Well, there's no sense worrying about it right now." Tess patted the seat next to her. "Stu's girlfriend and her team will be here in a little while, so let's have some coffee and decide what to do about Robin."

Janice sat in the seat Tess indicated. Winnie poured her some coffee.

"Thank you, Winnie," she said, then turned to Tess. "What do you mean? What's to decide? Surely you don't still suspect Robin. She was telling the truth about her dog." She motioned to LuAnn, who was cuddling Cecille like a baby. The dog let out a contented sigh.

"I admit, at first I did suspect her because I thought she didn't really have a dog. And I was wrong." Tess smiled. "But if you tell anyone I said that, I'll deny it."

"Mum's the word." Janice raised her eyebrows. "And now that you know the truth?"

"I still can't put my finger on it, but doesn't it seem a little too coincidental that someone who is studying the Underground Railroad just happens to end up at our inn just a few weeks before the bones show up in the tunnel?" She shrugged.

"I don't think we can eliminate Robin as a suspect just yet. Although, I have to say, the more I get to know her, the more I'm hoping she's innocent."

Raising her coffee mug, LuAnn held Cecille tighter with one hand. "Hear, hear."

The kitchen door opened, and they glanced up to see Isaiah entering. "Sorry to intrude, but there's someone here to speak to one or all of you."

Janice's heart picked up speed. "Send her on in." This would be the first of Stuart's girlfriends since he was in high school that she would get to meet. She couldn't help but envision flowers, lace, and shopping for a mother-of-the-groom dress.

Isaiah turned and motioned for her to come in.

Only, "she" wasn't female. Standing in their kitchen was Karl Mannus, the anchor from Channel 8 news. Tess stood and limped to him, accepting his proffered hand. "Did we have an interview I wasn't aware of?"

The man gave her his thousand-watt smile. Janice had to admit, he was a looker, but Tess wasn't the sort to have her head turned by a pretty face.

"No, ma'am," he said. "I thought the three of you might want to comment on the arrest last night. Our sources say the offender was storing stolen goods here."

LuAnn snorted and joined Tess, Cecille still cradled in her arms. "You thought we might want to comment? Why would we?"

The man seemed nonplussed by the less-than-pleasant welcome. He reached forward and scratched Cecille behind the ear. She leaned into his hand and sighed.

"You'll be opening your inn soon, right?" he said. "It could be free advertising for your big opening."

Tess folded her arms across her chest. "Why on earth would we want to introduce our inn to folks by admitting we hired an electrician who used our inn to hide his contraband?"

"Your electrician?"

Janice cringed. Clearly, Tess had given the nosy newsman more information than he'd come in knowing. She stepped forward and stood by her two friends. Together they formed a human shield. "You know all you need to know. So, all we have to say is, 'no comment.'"

"That's right," Winnie chimed in from her place by the oven where she slid a pan of apple popovers into the oven. "*Nooo* comment."

"Well, thank you for your time, anyway."

Janice couldn't help but feel sorry for him. Not sorry enough to allow him to turn the inn's first real TV exposure into something negative, of course. But the least she could do was walk him to the door.

"These are beautiful pieces," he said as they walked through the front entryway area.

"Thank you. We think so."

"Will they go into the guest rooms?"

"Some will. We're getting the others appraised to sell."

"Oh?" His eyebrows rose as he moved toward a silver tea service sitting on one of the dressers. "This looks English. Actually, it looks Edwardian." His tone betrayed his excitement as he started to reach for a teapot, then turned. "May I?"

Janice didn't see the harm. "Sure."

He lifted it, turned it over, and released a slow whistle. "Is this a family heirloom?"

"It is, yes." He didn't need to know whose family heirloom it was.

He paused, then turned to her, replacing the pot. "Ma'am, if this is a piece you are selling," he said, excitement edging his voice, "this silver collection alone could bring you five figures."

Janice couldn't hold back a sharp breath. "What?"

"Do you even know what you have here?" There was awe in his tone. "This tea and coffee service is manufactured by Holland, Aldwinckle, & Slater."

Blinking, Janice stared at him with what she was almost positive wasn't the most intelligent of expressions.

"You don't know the company?"

She shook her head. "I'm sure LuAnn would. We're having it appraised this week."

"Where did it all come from?" He frowned as though he realized his curiosity wasn't professional. "I mean, if you don't mind my asking from a strictly personal curiosity."

She leveled her narrowed gaze at him. "So, this would be off the record?"

"Definitely."

"We bought a bed from a woman who had family history with the inn. She left us all of this stuff when she passed away."

His eyes widened, and he seemed at a loss for words. Janice almost wished her friends were present to witness the phenomenon of stunning a reporter into silence. "Well, it seems like providence smiled on you three."

"We were shocked and grateful." Janice was starting to relax. "To be honest, we weren't sure how we were going to open on time."

"Finances have been an issue, then?"

"Well, we're three retired women and two of us are widows. I was beginning to wonder if I could really stay in the partnership." She smiled. "But God worked all that out."

"You were considering selling out to the others?"

She shrugged. "I hadn't made any decision. But there was a lot of pressure not to continue. Neither of my children are really in favor of the whole venture."

The door opened and the archaeological team descended upon the inn amid the chaos of the cluttered entryway and construction noise coming from the third and fourth floors. In the middle of it all was Karl Mannus, his eyes sparkling as though he smelled an even better story than he'd dreamed of.

Janice could've kicked herself for allowing him to linger over the silver tea and coffee service, but she hoped her friends would forgive her when they heard the worth of the silver. Right now, she was focused on the familiar-looking young woman standing in front of her, holding out her hand. Her dark hair was pulled up into a bun and she wore a pair of Bermuda shorts, a pink plaid button-down shirt, and a pair of short tan boots.

"I'm Avi," she said, her smile beginning with her eyes.

"Janice Eastman," Janice said, as she looked into the pretty face of the young woman who might have captured her son's affections. She didn't want to blow this.

"Stuart has told me so much about you, Mrs. Eastman. It's wonderful to meet you."

"Likewise."

LuAnn and Tess came from the kitchen, LuAnn, of course, still carrying her new little friend. Before Janice could make introductions, Cecille started to wiggle in LuAnn's arms.

"What's the matter, little girl?" LuAnn asked. "Do you want down?"

Laughter bubbled from Avi as the dog sprinted to her. Avi scooped her up and continued to giggle as Cecille washed her face with her tongue. "Cecille, baby! Auntie's missed you. Yes, I have."

LuAnn, Tess, and Janice exchanged confused gazes. Then slowly, they came to the same conclusion: Avi, working at the university in Athens, was Robin's sister.

CHAPTER FIFTEEN

"Avi!" Robin entered the room, her clothing covered in sawdust. "You made it!"

Tess leaned in close to Janice. "You have to wonder why she didn't tell us the archaeologist coming from the university is her sister."

Janice couldn't disagree. They'd sat together over breakfast, so she'd had plenty of time to reveal the information. Not to mention they'd babysat her dog all morning. A heads-up might have been in order. Robin had to have known her sister was coming. And if that were the case, she had deliberately withheld the information. Had Tess's suspicion this whole time been justified after all?

"Mrs. Eastman," Robin said, laughter bubbling from deep inside of her. "Finally, you've met my sister."

"Yes, apparently."

Robin laughed again and threw her arm around Janice's shoulders. "Don't be mad at me, please. Avi made me promise not to say anything until Stuart was ready to spill the beans on their relationship."

Or maybe she was exactly who she said she was.

Avi handed Cecille to Robin and turned to the Inn Crowd. "So, how do we do this? Can we see the tunnel and get set up?"

At some point during the hoopla and introductions, Tess disappeared and came back carrying a small basket. "Ms. Washington will show you all down there. But first, put your phones right in here. You can get them back when you leave." She held the basket out to Avi.

She stared in disbelief at Tess. "You're not serious?"

"As two feet of snow in summer."

Avi turned to Janice. "We aren't allowed to take photos or film? Not even for teaching purposes?"

Robin sent her sister a warning look. "Avi..."

A wave of compassion spread across Janice's chest at the disappointment marring Avi's face. She might have relented if Tess hadn't spoken up first. "No photos," she said firmly. "No devices of any kind."

Robin shifted, clearly uncomfortable for her sister. "If you guys will excuse me, I have to get back to work." She handed Cecille back to LuAnn and waved at Avi as she headed toward the stairs.

Avi pulled her phone from her back pocket and turned to her team. "Okay, guys, cough 'em up. If anyone brought two phones and decides to get cute, you should know I'll drop you from my classes in a heartbeat for defying our hosts' wishes."

Respect for the young woman rose in Janice's heart. Maybe Stuart had finally found the woman who was worthy of him.

"How long will you need down there, do you think?" LuAnn asked.

Avi drew in a breath and exhaled. "I'm not sure. Do you have a time limit in mind for us?" She smiled, sweeping the three of them with her gaze. "I don't want to wear out our welcome."

Her humility clearly impressed Tess. She shrugged and looked to Janice and LuAnn.

Janice shook her head. "I don't think it matters as long as you don't stay past quitting time for the crew."

"Agreed," said LuAnn.

"You have my word." Avi smiled at Janice. "It's truly a pleasure meeting you, ma'am."

"And you too." Janice had to force herself not to gush and overshare. She was just so happy to meet a woman who had caught Stuart's eye.

They watched the archaeology team follow Winnie to the basement steps. Tess laughed, turning to Janice. "That girl has it bad for Stuart."

"How can you tell?" Janice asked, hope rising strong.

LuAnn gave a laugh of her own. "She's bending over backward to comply with our requests, even though it was pretty clear she wanted to take photos or film the tunnel. Plus, she was laying it on pretty thick with the mother of her boyfriend."

Janice grinned. "Maybe you're right. Let's just hope Stuart feels the same way."

LuAnn set Cecille on the floor. "We're going to get online and try to find an appraiser so we can get these things out of here." She headed toward the office, leaving Tess and Janice behind.

At the mention of the appraiser, Janice recalled her conversation with Karl Mannus. Just as she was about to call LuAnn back so she could tell them they might be sitting on an even bigger gold mine than they knew, the front door opened and a young man rushed in.

"Can we help you?" Tess asked.

Breathless, the twenty-something nodded. "I'm with the archaeologists here to look for bone fragments. Dr. Rogers is going to kill me." He seemed genuinely distressed. Janice couldn't help but feel a touch of concern. Was Avi... not nice?

"Come with me," she said. "I'll take you to them."

"Thank you," he breathed, sounding relieved.

"Why were you later than the others?" she asked. "I thought the team drove together."

"We did. I got hung up outside talking to some guy with big teeth."

Alarm seized Janice. She knew exactly whose teeth he was talking about. "Did he ask questions about the inn?"

"Yeah, he wanted to know what we were doing here. I told him we were working on plumbing." He grinned an adorable, boyish grin that made him look eighteen years old.

Janice laughed. "Did he believe it?"

"Nah, he wore me down. He knows the guy working on the pipes here, so he didn't buy it. Sorry."

"Well, you tried. Did you give him anything worthwhile?" Janice took the last step and turned to look at her companion.

"I just told him we were looking for bone fragments from a bunch of old bones we picked up last week." He shrugged, then hesitated and frowned. "Was that too much?"

Well, goodness gracious goat. Karl had hit the jackpot if he wanted to report on the inn. First, she'd told him all about the antiques and now he knew about the bones.

She was afraid they should've just given him the statement about James's arrest in the first place. Now, he had a lot of information they weren't ready to share with the world. And she'd promised not to withhold anything from her friends. She had no choice but to confess before they were blindsided by the six o'clock news.

Thirty minutes later, the three friends still sat around the table, recovering from the knowledge that, despite their best efforts, they might not be able to keep the discovery of the bones a secret. LuAnn and Tess were less concerned with Janice's conversation about the antiques than they were the bones story.

"I'm never watching that station again," LuAnn said emphatically.

"What a creep," Tess said. "And I've always liked watching him. I wonder how many other stories he's gotten through deception and trickery."

LuAnn scowled. "Well, it certainly does explain why he rose to anchor so quickly. Remember, he started out as a field reporter. If he weren't so good-looking..."

"Well, you know he's not going to pass up a juicy story about finding ancient bones in an old tunnel that was once used for the Underground Railroad."

Tess clenched her jaw. "Opportunist."

LuAnn sighed and pushed up from the table. "Well, there's nothing we can do about this now. Let's just do what we need to do for the day. I'm going to keep trying to find an appraiser."

"You're right, there's nothing we can do about it," Tess conceded. "But we still don't have to like it."

After a little while, LuAnn returned to the kitchen with little Cecille prancing along behind her.

"Any luck finding an appraiser, Lu?" Janice asked.

With a sigh, LuAnn shook her head and dropped into a chair. "I put in a couple of calls. One of them was in Columbus. So, we'll see."

"Well, while it's just us here, I think we need to discuss the elephant in the inn," Tess said.

LuAnn nodded, walking to the sink to refill Cecille's water dish. "There are so many elephants in this inn, we have a whole circus act to wade through."

"I'm talking about Robin sleeping in her car. What are we going to do about that?" Tess winced a little as she shifted her leg on the chair.

"And it can't be good for Cecille either," LuAnn said.

Janice wondered if her friend was more concerned about Robin or about the dog. She had a hunch it might just be the latter.

"Well," Janice said, "can we let her spend the night in one of the second-floor rooms?"

Tess pressed her lips together as LuAnn spoke up. "Alone? I'm not sure I'd even stay in this old building alone." She grinned at Janice. "And I know for sure you wouldn't."

"You're not wrong there." Janice chuckled.

"I'm not so sure we should leave the inn unattended at night anyway," Tess said. "We know the Steinway is worth an impressive five figures. And if Karl Mannus knows what he's talking about, the tea service could be too. The question is, what do we do about security now that we have so many items that are worth securing?"

"Do you think we should get an alarm?" Janice had never had a lot of luck with those things. When they installed them at the church, the police were alerted and showed up at least twice a week because she couldn't get the code to work right.

"I thought about that," Tess said. "But if we put alarms on the doors, they'll be tripped anytime a guest goes out after we set it. What if someone goes out for snacks in the middle of the night? Or fresh air?"

Janice nodded. "Good point."

"Besides," LuAnn said with a grin, "you know Janice's history with alarm systems."

Tess chuckled. "The police will thank us for not choosing that solution. What about a security guard? At least for now, while we have all of these things still in plain view."

"I could ask Randy if he knows of anyone who might want an overnight position for a couple of weeks—or maybe even longer," Janice offered. "Maybe until we're up and running with several guests every night?" They would have an overnight desk clerk once the inn could support one. That should help, but until then they needed a way to keep the inn secure.

"That sounds like the best solution to me," Tess said.

"I agree," Lu said. She drew a breath and exhaled, standing. "Well, we'd best get into the living room and get busy. Those books aren't going to put themselves away."

They spent the rest of the morning stuffing books into the shelves. By the time they'd emptied the last box and broken it down, Avi and her team emerged from the tunnels. Their faces showed disappointment.

"No luck on finding the bone fragments?" Janice asked, her arms full of flattened boxes on the way out to the industrial trash bin outside the kitchen door.

Avi shook her head. "We scoured every inch of that tunnel. Whoever dug up the bones must have left them where they were buried." She frowned as if in thought. "It just doesn't seem right to me."

"What do you mean, honey?"

She shrugged, and Janice was surprised to see emotion in her green eyes. "I know the bones aren't the actual person, but a hundred and fifty years ago, he was a human being with a family and love and someone believed he was worthwhile. Worth loving." She shook her head.

Janice studied the young woman's face as she spoke with such passion. "You take your work very seriously." A person would think she was speaking about someone she knew.

"It's not just work to me. They aren't just bones." She captured Janice's gaze, and there was no denying the earnestness that reached deep inside of Avi. "Every set of bones we uncover represents someone who lived." She shrugged again and seemed to gather her emotions back to her chest. "I think they should be respected, and that's what I try to teach my students."

Her gaze travelled to the boxes in Janice's arms. "Let me help with those while the others pack up the van."

Gladly, Janice relinquished the bulky load and led her through the kitchen to the back door.

"This inn really is remarkable," Avi said, stuffing the boxes into the Dumpster. "I'd love to learn more about its history."

"Well, I can't promise you we'll find more bones," Janice said. The very thought made her shudder. "But I'll discuss it with my friends, and perhaps we can give you the full tour one day soon."

"Thank you, Mrs. Eastman." Avi smiled, holding the door open so Janice could precede her back inside. "I'd love that."

"Please, just call me Janice."

Winnie had set platters of pastries and a pot of coffee on the table for the archaeology team, and LuAnn and Tess had joined them in the kitchen. The four students sat around the table. Their laughter reminded Janice of her children during their high school and early college years, when friends accompanied them home and filled the house with laughter and games, while they emptied her kitchen of food and drinks.

She smiled as memories washed over her, and suddenly she envisioned the day Larry would be bringing his friends home to Stacy. She wondered if Stuart would ever have the same joy.

She cast a glance at Avi as she declined pastries but accepted coffee. "You didn't have to make snacks."

"We appreciate it though." The young man who had come in late held up his pastry. "Ms. Washington, these are the most *fantastalicious* apple turnovers I've ever had. But don't tell my mom!"

Clearly pleased with the praise, Winnie smiled. "You kids take the leftovers with you." She cut a sly glance to Avi. "I'll box up a couple for you to take to Dr. Eastman."

Janice could have kissed the cook at giving her an opening to discuss their relationship without being obvious. "Oh, will you be seeing Stuart today?"

Avi's cheeks reddened at the mention of Stuart. She clearly did care about him. That caused Janice's heart to swell, and she couldn't help but wonder if perhaps she really was looking at her future daughter-in-law.

But Avi shook her head. "He has appointments all day, and I have plans with my mother while she's still in town."

"Robin mentioned your mother is staying with you while she's in the area." Janice smiled. "Maybe Robin won't have to work as much the next time she comes for a visit."

Avi chuckled. "It's more about her having the dog, I think. Mom's allergic." She pushed away from the table. "Okay, gang, it's time we finished things up and hit the road."

By lunchtime, the team had gone, and things quieted down at the inn. LuAnn had heard back from the auction houses she'd contacted, but no one could get to the inn for an appraisal for two weeks.

"Where are we going to put all these things in the meantime?" Tess asked, her helpless expression mirroring Janice's thoughts.

LuAnn shrugged and released a sigh. "I don't know. Maybe we should rent a storage unit."

Janice echoed LuAnn's sigh. "We'll probably have to."

"I'm sure Michael can get a couple of men together to get it moved," Tess said.

"We have to hire someone anyway," LuAnn agreed. "I'd rather pay one of our own and feel confident these things will be well cared for."

"Agreed." Janice glanced at the piano. "Should we just leave that be? It looks beautiful where it is."

"Yes!" Tess said.

It would be the following day before Michael could pull a small crew together and pick up the antiques, so the women decided to spend one more night in the inn to watch over things. If they were being honest, Janice knew that at the back of their minds, was the fact that Robin had slept in her car the night before. They would offer her the Maple and Mum room and since LuAnn and Tess were used to rooming together, they decided to double up in the honeymoon suite.

When the crew knocked off at five thirty, Robin came to collect Cecille from LuAnn. She found them upstairs hanging wall decorations and adding lamps to the three second-floor rooms. "Hello?" she said, tapping on the door to the honeymoon suite. Janice was eyeballing a wall clock as LuAnn attempted to hang it straight.

"Come in," Tess said. Cecille hopped off a chair in the corner and ran to her owner. Robin scooped up the dog. "Were you a good girl today?" she cooed.

LuAnn glanced over her shoulder, keeping her hands on the clock. "She was perfect."

"That's perfect too," Janice said. "Leave it."

"Thank you all for keeping Cecille today." Robin looked exhausted, and her clothing and skin were covered in a layer of dust. Janice's heart went out to her. Imagine trying to get a good night's sleep all scrunched up in your car. Her body ached just thinking about it.

"How long will it be before your pipes are fixed?" she asked.

Robin shrugged. "The super said not today, and that's all he would tell me. So it could be as early as tomorrow and as long as who-knows-when." She smiled to include them all. "Are you worrying about me? Listen, don't. I've been traveling alone and fending for myself since I was a crazy kid."

"Oh, Robin. Don't be silly." Tess waved a hand. "Three of these rooms are ready to sleep in. We can't rest well if we know you're sleeping in your car. Marietta is a nice, safe town, but a woman alone like that isn't safe anywhere. Especially on a hot summer night when you'll have to leave your windows down or suffocate."

Janice hadn't even thought about the windows. Her stomach clenched just imagining all the things that could happen to their new friend.

"Oh, no. Really, please don't be that nice to me. You really, really don't have to and to be honest, I'm starting to feel like I'm taking advantage of your generosity. Staying in this beautiful inn would just be too much."

"You would be doing us a favor," LuAnn said.

Janice turned to her with a frown. As much as she appreciated LuAnn's attempt to ease Robin's conscience, she couldn't fathom how on earth she could possibly think the intelligent young woman would fall for that one. Clearly, it was they who were doing her the favor.

"That's right." Tess jumped on the deceptive bandwagon, so Janice felt she had no choice but to agree with them.

"We would definitely appreciate it if you'd stay. We—um—"

"Those antiques are very expensive. We're not comfortable leaving them overnight with the inn empty."

Robin's eyes widened, and understanding seemed to dawn in her expression. "Oh. Do you want me to keep an eye on them? That's different. I can just sleep on the couch downstairs, though. I definitely don't need to take up one of the rooms before you even have a chance to book a guest."

Janice believed Robin. The low-maintenance young woman would likely be comfortable and at ease anywhere she landed.

"We're not leaving you alone here, either," Tess said as though Robin hadn't spoken. Her face took on that determination and no-arguments look that had worked well for her when she taught a group of rowdy teenagers in their first year of college, using her class to fulfill an elective credit. "LuAnn and I are taking this suite. Janice's things are already in the Lily and

Lace room so she'll stay there, and you can have the other room. And if you want to pay for your room, feel free to make them all up in the morning."

"Tess!" Janice said. "She's our guest."

Robin laughed, shaking her head. "No, Mrs. Eastman. She knows I'd never agree to your sweet offer without doing my part. Not only will I get the rooms spick-and-span in the morning, I'm cooking supper tonight. I noticed there's a grill out back. Be prepared to eat the most scrumptious burgers of your lives."

"Wonderful," Janice said, clapping her hands. "And while we eat, you'll tell us all about how Stuart and your sister met."

She noticed hesitance in Robin's eyes at the suggestion, but she could put on a no-nonsense face as well as Tess could, so she did. "Now, I forgive you for keeping me in the dark about it before I knew Stuart had a girlfriend. But I've met her now and like her as well as I can after such a short meeting, so I need information my son is never going to offer up unless he's under some sort of pain medication, which I don't see happening any time soon."

"Well, if I tell you how they met you have to promise not to throw me under the bus."

"Scout's honor."

Robin held out her hand. "Then it's a deal."

CHAPTER SIXTEEN

It was almost eleven by the time Janice pulled on her pajamas and climbed into bed. She clicked on the television to the news. It had been such a full day, starting a full hour earlier than normal for her. When Karl Mannus's big, toothy smile and perfect hair showed up on the screen, she perked up. Her heart sank as he led off with James's arrest.

She closed her eyes. *Please, please, please don't mention the bones. Please don't mention the bones.*

"And now, another story about the Wayfarers Inn." She opened her eyes as he continued. "Against the wishes of many Marietta residents, three local women purchased the building two months ago and have been working furiously to get the renovations completed to open in time for the Sternwheel Festival next month."

Incensed, Janice pushed up to sit on the edge of the bed. They had told him they didn't want to comment. And what did he mean by *Against the wishes of many Marietta residents?* He made it sound like they were big city jerks coming to small-town America to tear down a beloved historic building and build a mall. Besides, she and Tess were residents of Marietta themselves.

But that wasn't the worst part of the story. Her heart jumped into overdrive as she saw footage of the inn. Although they didn't show her full face, there she was, in the entryway, smack-dab in the middle of the beautiful antiques, spilling her guts to the Judas standing over her.

He'd said her comments were off the record. He'd even pretended to be interested in the silver. Could they sue? And where had the cameraman been? Hiding in the bushes?

He went on to include the story of the woman in Athens who left them the antiques. "The incredible gift that one of the women attributes to God includes many pieces that belonged to the inn at the turn of the twentieth century when it was originally named Wayfarers Inn. I stood in the middle of the beautiful pieces and, as a lover of antiques, I have to tell you folks, I was blown away. These pieces are perfectly preserved and some of the highest quality of antiques I've ever seen. I'm definitely getting my bid in when they are put up for auction."

Janice blew out a breath she didn't even know she was holding. It could've been worse.

A knock at her door made her jump and as the station switched to a commercial, she clicked the TV off. She was never watching that liar again. *Off the record*, her left hind foot.

"Come in."

"Don't pretend you didn't see the news," Tess said walking into the room. She sat on the edge of Janice's bed with a sigh.

Janice still couldn't believe she'd been so foolish. "I feel just awful. He promised anything I said was off the record. How could I have known he couldn't be trusted? He has such an honest face."

LuAnn opened the door and peeked her head in. She looked at Tess. "I heard you leave the room. I thought I'd find you here."

Tess grinned at LuAnn. "Janice was just saying she didn't know Karl Mannus couldn't be trusted."

Defenses rising, Janice lifted her chin. "Well, he did say 'off the record.'"

LuAnn gave her a sympathetic smile. "He knew how to get you to open up. We don't blame you."

"So, he recognized a sucker when he saw one," Janice said with a self-recriminating sigh.

"Oh, don't be too hard on yourself," Tess said. "And what's the worst that can happen? People know about the antiques? Maybe we'll get more people to show up to the auction."

"That's true." LuAnn nodded. "He probably gave us free publicity for the inn too."

Janice was relieved that her wonderful friends were being so supportive.

"And he got in a plug for God too," LuAnn said, smiling. "That makes me happy."

Tess covered a yawn with the back of her hand. "Well, morning's going to come early." She nudged Janice. "Don't feel bad, Janice. He could've roped any one of us in with that deceptively honest face."

Tess and LuAnn returned to their room, and Janice slid back under the covers and switched off the lamp. "Lord," she whispered, "please set a watch over my mouth from here on out."

As she dozed off, she thought about that interview and prayed again. "Please protect the inn and the antiques."

Janice woke with a start to the sound of thumping and moving around above her. She lay in the darkness, staring at the ceiling, her heart pounding in her ears. The familiar feeling of hot and cold fear wound through her stomach, up her chest, and down her arms.

Had James made bail and come back to find more goods he'd hidden? If he'd found a secret room they'd had no idea existed, wasn't it possible he'd found a hiding spot upstairs as well?

Fear caught her in its paralyzing grip as her thoughts evolved from James retrieving the rest of his loot to more nefarious motives. What if he'd seen their cars out front and decided to punish them for getting him arrested in the first place?

Or what if he'd seen the newscast and decided to pick up a few of the antiques for himself? There were certainly things that were small enough for him to get out of the inn without too much effort—the coffee and tea service, for instance. Although, thankfully, Karl Mannus hadn't mentioned them, nor had the camera caught them close up.

That didn't explain what he'd be doing on the third floor, though.

She reached for her phone on the table by the bed, then remembered with a groan that she'd forgotten it downstairs earlier and had decided to leave it until morning.

Janice knew she had to do something. She couldn't just lie there wallowing in fear while her friends and Robin were sleeping. But what could she do without a phone to call the police?

Slowly she got out of bed and looked around for a weapon. Where was a heavy wooden bat when you needed one? Helplessness washed over her until her gaze landed on her purse. Her heart jumped as she picked it up from the chair in the corner and fished around inside. She pulled out a sample bottle of hair spray and studied it for only a second before making her decision.

Lawrence had never wanted her to own pepper spray. He'd felt it would be more of a danger for her than a help if she ever found herself face-to-face with a mugger. But she'd taken her own initiative by picking up this little can of hair spray for ninety-nine cents. She couldn't knock someone senseless with it, but a big squirt in the eyeballs would stop a bad person cold. She knew the pain firsthand, as many times as she'd sprayed the stuff into her own eyes while fixing her hair for church.

She thought about taking a moment for an earnest prayer, but the thumping from above grew stronger and she knew the intruder could be just minutes away from descending the steps to do who knew what.

It was up to her to save her friends, so she prayed as she walked.

Janice stopped, a frown on her face, when she reached the hallway. There was a glow coming from the Maple and Mums room. She made a fast decision to knock on Robin's door. Maybe she had her phone and they could call 911.

As she reached the room, she saw that the door was slightly cracked so she tapped. No answer. She knocked a little harder. Still there was nothing from inside except a little yip from Cecille. Though she was uncomfortable invading someone's privacy, another series of thumpings from above convinced her. She stepped into the room and looked around. It was clear from the open bathroom door that there was no one here. Pausing by the bed, she scratched the dog behind the ears. Cecille jumped up and, as she stepped to the edge of the bed, her paw landed on the keyboard of Robin's open laptop, waking up the screen.

Janice stopped, all at once confused, then troubled. Then, as the full weight of clarity forced itself on her mind, heartbreak settled over her. The computer's wallpaper staring back at her was the woman and child in the photograph she'd found with the skeleton. Tess had been right about Robin all along.

Oh, Robin. I so wanted to believe in you.

Disheartened, she moved from Robin's room and ascended the steps to the third floor, keeping her senses alert as she looked up, her hand wrapped tightly around the hair spray sample. With her finger on the nozzle, she took the last step, just as she heard another series of thumping louder than before but still clearly above her. The intruder—was it Robin?— was on the fourth floor, not this one.

Gathering a breath, trying desperately to quell the fear churning and burning inside her stomach, Janice climbed the steps between the third and fourth floors. Her mind kept replaying the last few days since Robin had first walked into the living room after work. Coincidentally or not so coincidentally a few hours after Janice had discovered the bones and photo.

Had she played them all like fiddles?

Janice heard voices as she reached the top of the stairs. Did Robin have an accomplice? She knew she couldn't stop out here in the open, so she forced her legs to carry her forward, following the sound.

The murmur of tense voices again brought her back to the seriousness of the present situation. She listened closer. Were they arguing? And . . . the voices were coming from her rooms!

She took a couple of tentative, tiptoe steps, then peeked around the edge of the doorframe. A sense of urgency rose in her as she saw Robin, her hands planted on her hips, confronting the intruder, who wore a white mask covering his nose and mouth, and a ball cap on his head. Janice saw the man suddenly reach for Robin, as though he were about to accost her.

Before she knew what she was doing, she jumped from the doorway and rushed toward the man, "Oh, no you don't, buster!" She lunged at him, spraying wildly as he yelled.

"Mom!"

"Mrs. Eastman!"

"Mom! Stop spraying me!"

November 1858

Prudence and Cecille had been at the inn for two days, hiding in its secret basement. The entrance to the basement was hidden in a panel in the wall just above them, and the entrance to the tunnel that would eventually take them under the street all the way to the river was hidden right here in Cecille's room. The owner of the inn had the forethought to have a servant bell installed in the hallway as an emergency alert should danger be imminent.

She sat in a rocking chair in Cecille's room, sewing fabric together for baby diapers and sitting watch over Cecille and Willa as they slept. In the last two days, when she hadn't been upstairs at the inn fulfilling her duties so she didn't raise suspicion among the guests and other employees, she had set herself to the task of sewing tiny gowns and diapers for Willa, using sheets from the linen closet with Mr. Siloam's permission. During their time together, Cecille had also confirmed that Rafe Wimber was the father of both of the children she'd birthed.

Prudence slept in one of the eight secret rooms, and as uncomfortable as she was in such close proximity to Logan, or any man not her husband, he slept on the other side of the narrow hallway.

It wasn't difficult to discern Mr. Wimber's devotion to Cecille. If not love, it was most certainly high regard and affection.

A loud knock on the door startled Prudence and she stood quickly, dumping her sewing onto the floor. "Yes?"

The sound had awakened Cecille, and her eyes were round with fright as she clutched her baby tightly against her breast.

"Do not be afraid," Prudence reassured. "It is only Mr. Siloam."

He knocked again. "Mrs. Willard, I must speak with you."

Hearing his urgent tone, Prudence slid open the lock and opened the door. Jason stood with him.

At the first sight in two days of her husband, Prudence melted into his arms, heedless of their audience. "Thee are a sight for sore eyes, dear."

"And thee as well, my love."

Logan Wimber, apparently drawn by the knocking and voices, had left his room and stood behind Jason. "What's going on?" he asked.

At the same time Prudence asked Jason, "What is thee doing here?"

"Mrs. Willard," Mr. Siloam said, his face somber. "We have no choice but to move the woman and child tonight."

"What has happened?"

"Dear one," Jason said, "Rafe Wimber and his men searched our home tonight. He grew suspicious when he discovered the things thee sewed for our baby." He swallowed hard. "Before."

Feeling his sense of loss still over the death of their last child, she touched his arm. "Continue."

"He inquired as to thy whereabouts, and I told him thee is employed at the inn. It seemed the proper thing to do."

He had done the right thing. It was better to tell a verifiable story than to make up a lie Mr. Wimber could easily have investigated.

"And why does this mean we have to move with such haste? Cecille is only now beginning to gain her strength."

Jason took Prudence by the arms and met her gaze firmly. "I followed Rafe and two of his men as they searched other houses. I do not believe the sheriff is aware of these house searches, as he was not present."

"That's almost certain," Logan said, speaking from behind Jason. "My brother has no intention of having me arrested. When he catches up to us, he will take Cecille and the baby back to Wimber plantation and snatch Willa from Cecille's arms for his wife. If I make it alive back to my home, he'll hang me as a traitor to the family."

Jason gripped Prudence's arms more tightly. "I heard them talking."

Mr. Siloam narrowed his gaze at Jason. "What did you overhear?"

"Mr. Wimber mentioned something about a woman of…ill repute…I am sorry to mention such a woman in your gentle presence, ladies."

"Please, tell me the rest." With all the ugliness she'd been forced to witness during the past few years, he still tried to protect her sensibilities and virtues. How she loved him.

"While he was in the saloon last night, the woman claimed she once held employment here at the inn but was removed from her position as maid when she was caught with a male guest...oh, I am sorry."

Irritation born of urgency flooded Prudence. "Jason, please. I am not a child, nor am I an unmarried woman. Hurry, and tell me the rest."

He nodded. "Yes, of course. This woman gave him information of a secret entrance to these rooms. She claims to have witnessed you, Prudence, opening the panel upstairs."

Prudence gasped, feeling the blood drain from her face. If the wrong person discovered the rooms, this would no longer be a viable station—not to mention that the owner of the inn, Mr. Siloam, and Prudence, herself, would be arrested. They must not allow that to happen.

Mr. Siloam grabbed the carpetbag from the corner and tossed it into the middle of the room. "Get Cecille's things packed, quickly. There is a wagon waiting at the tunnel exit by the river."

Prudence began to stuff Cecille's meager belongings, along with the tiny pieces of clothing she had sewn, into the bag as she spoke. "But where will she go? No one is expecting her arrival, and you said yourself the steamboat won't be back this way for a couple of weeks."

"I have a map for Mr. Wimber to follow to the next station five miles from here. Since the woman must be transported in the wagon, I would like for you to accompany them. I must be here in case Rafe Wimber arrives."

Jason stepped forward. "I'll be the one to drive the wagon."

There would be no arguing with him, and Prudence wouldn't have wanted to. But she had no intention of allowing him to go alone. "That will bring me comfort, Husband."

Mr. Siloam stepped into the hallway, urging haste.

Jason glowered, clearly intending for her to remain behind, but she sent him a silent plea. She would insist if necessary, but she did not want to show a lack of respect for her husband in front of strangers.

Cecille had remained silent the entire time, but now she stood on shaky legs, clad in her nightgown. Jason turned immediately away and stepped into the hallway with Mr. Siloam. Nonplussed, Mr. Wimber closed the distance and swept Cecille and the baby into his arms.

"I—I can walk."

"Shh. It'll be quicker this way."

His tenderness touched Prudence, and it was clear now that he loved her very much. Cecille laid her head against his shoulder, and the show of utter trust told Prudence that Cecille loved this man as well. In Canada they could be married.

Jason grabbed Cecille's bag and the bedding and moved into the hallway. Prudence followed, closing the door behind them.

Just as they reached the tunnel exit, Prudence heard the faint sound of the bell, which could only mean one thing.

Rafe Wimber had arrived.

CHAPTER SEVENTEEN

J anice stared, speechless, at her son until finally she found her voice. "You put the bones in the basement?" she asked, hardly able to bear the thought of what his answer would be.

He frowned. "What? No, Ma! Why would I do that?"

"Don't lie to me. I want to know right this minute why you've been breaking into the inn."

"I haven't exactly been breaking in," he said, his lips curving into a smile. "Aunt Tess gave me a copy of the basement key."

Narrowing her gaze, Janice studied his face. Except for a little redness from the minuscule amount of hair spray that actually reached its target, his eyes were completely empty of deception. She had always been able to tell when one of her children wasn't being honest. She folded her arms across her chest. "Start talking, mister. What's going on?"

"Don't you notice anything different about your room?"

Janice glanced around, suddenly drew in a sharp breath, and walked to the fireplace—the one that wasn't there before. The fireplaces had been pulled out of the walls prior to the three of them purchasing the inn.

"You did this? Surely, you didn't. You don't know how..." She knew she was rambling but couldn't seem to help herself. "I don't know what to say, Stuey."

"As far back as I can remember, you've wanted a fireplace."

He was right. The parsonage had all electric heat, but Janice had always loved a stone fireplace. She tried, two or three times over the years, to persuade Lawrence to buy their own home or build one of their own, but he'd always believed living in the parsonage kept him accessible to his congregation. Janice had always secretly believed he didn't want to spend the time or money on the upkeep of their own home. And while she couldn't necessarily blame him, she'd always dreamed of having a stone fireplace. She was sure that, each winter, she had voiced her regret that she couldn't enjoy a cozy fire or hang the children's stocking from a mantel.

"When I first saw that your room used to have one, I knew I could learn how to put one in for you. I didn't plan for you to find out this way. I envisioned balloons and snacks." He grinned.

A sense of wonder flooded over Janice as she stepped forward to the gray stone fireplace. She could see it in the wintertime, the way she'd always envisioned one just like this, lit up with flames, warming her as she sat in front of it, her Bible in her lap. "Stu," she breathed, "I don't know what to say."

Turning, she allowed herself to be folded into his arms. When she pulled away, she saw Robin grinning at the show of affection between them, and the memory of what she'd seen downstairs flooded back over her, dampening her joy.

Robin stepped forward and gave Janice a hug. "I'm so happy for you, Mrs. Eastman."

Stuart laughed. "I've been accosted twice in one night."

Janice tried not to stiffen in Robin's arms. But she knew her quick pat and equally quick step backward confused Robin as she pulled away with a small frown.

"What do you mean you were accosted twice?" Janice asked.

Robin smiled, though it didn't quite reach her eyes and barely dented her cheeks at all. "I heard something upstairs and thought someone had broken in." She shrugged. "The surgical mask he was wearing to keep out the dust didn't help."

She should talk! If anyone was guilty of breaking in it was her. Breaking into their hearts when she was trying to sabotage their efforts. At least Stuart was there under noble motives.

"I hear you met someone today, Ma." Stuart's eyes scanned her face. "What'd you think of Avi?"

Janice smiled. "She's lovely." But she had to remember that she'd thought Robin was lovely too. Oh, she felt so foolish and angry that she'd been duped. Were the sisters in this together? She didn't see how on earth they couldn't be.

"I'm glad you like her. This wasn't the way I'd envisioned introducing the two of you, though."

Robin laughed. "Were you planning balloons and snacks for that reveal too?"

Janice forced a smile and clamped her mouth shut so she didn't say too much. She was so close to confronting Robin about the screen saver, but she knew she had to discuss the situation with Tess and LuAnn first, especially in light of Stuart's relationship with Avi, who might be nothing more than an accomplice using her son to gain access to the inn.

Stuart yawned and his eyes watered, and Janice realized he must've been working through the night. "Son, you'd better get home and get some rest."

He nodded. "I was just getting ready to when Robin came in wielding that little billy club."

For the first time, Janice noticed what was in Robin's hand. Robin gave her a sheepish smile. "For protection when I'm alone. It pops out into a stick."

"Light saber." Stuart's gaze on Robin's face was one of true admiration. Were his affections caught between the sisters? Sisters in crime at that.

"Well, since I know your mother and her friends aren't in danger from a burglar, I guess I can go back to bed. I have to be up in"—she glanced at her watch and groaned—"an hour. I hope Cecille doesn't have to go out."

"I'm going to take off too," Stuart said. "I have Stace schedule appointments later in the day after the nights I'm here, so I can sleep a few hours before I go in."

"Stacy knew about this too?"

"Just her and Aunt Tess. I swore them to secrecy and didn't even tell Aunt Lu. I'm gonna have to give her free clinic visits for the rest of her life to make up for keeping her in the dark."

"Tess should win an Oscar for her performance when James Avery told me he'd seen you around the inn at night. She even let LuAnn write your name down as a suspect."

He frowned. "A suspect for what?"

"Well, we're still trying to figure out who put the bones in the tunnel. I found a photograph with them, so someone wanted us to figure it out. We just don't know who or why. We've been looking in Prudence Willard's journal and found a couple of entries that might be referring to the woman in the photo. But it's hard to know for sure."

"You three..." He slung his arm around her and pulled her sideways for a tight hug. As he did, Janice realized that Robin was still standing in the doorway. Her eyes were as big as saucers, and she turned and fled.

Janice knew there was no point in trying to go back to sleep. Drawn to the journal, she turned to the pages that they'd read before about the woman who was helped by L. Wimber. She began to read on, farther than they'd had a chance to read all together.

> We believed we were going to perish. R. Wimber had been clever. He knew Jason was following them, and when Jason veered off to warn us at RH, he sent his men on to continue the searches and followed him. He watched as Siloam had the wagon moved and when we exited the tunnel, he was waiting.

Janice heard a knock on the door and dragged herself away from the journal. Tess stood there in her nightgown. "So, you found out about your little surprise?" she asked.

Janice opened the door wider for her to come in. "I did." She grinned. "So much for us not keeping secrets from each other. I would like to know something, though. Are you the one who took the memory card out of my hidden camera?"

Tess walked to the chair in the corner, her limp much less noticeable. She grinned. "As you might recall, I never denied it."

"I'm going to remember that handy trick next time you ask me something. How did you know I found out about Stuart?"

"Who could sleep with all the noise? I heard you and Robin talking in the hallway a little while ago."

Frowning, Janice shook her head. "I wasn't talking to her. She must've been on the phone." Janice pulled in a breath. "I think we'd better wake up Lu."

Ten minutes later, they all sat in the sitting area of the honeymoon suite while Janice revealed that she'd seen the same photograph on Robin's computer.

"I knew there was more to that girl than meets the eye," Tess said. "Now we just need to figure out her motive."

"Don't you think we should ask Robin flat out?" LuAnn said. "I still like her a lot, and it's not like she killed the person whose remains we discovered." She turned to Tess. "And she did have a dog, so now we don't even have reason to believe she lied about anything."

Janice knew she had a point, but Stuart's obvious affection for both Robin and Avi bothered her. "What about the sister? Don't you think it's too much of a coincidence that she's an archaeologist and also somehow connected to that photograph?"

LuAnn stood and walked to the door. "I think we should give Robin a chance to explain herself."

Reluctantly Tess agreed, so Janice felt she had no choice but to go along with the plan.

When LuAnn returned a couple of minutes later, she was alone.

"Is Robin coming?"

She shook her head. "She's gone and took all of her things with her."

Bleary-eyed from lack of sleep, Janice, Tess, and LuAnn sat at the kitchen table, a pot of coffee between them, eating leftover pastries and fruit for their breakfast. Janice rested her chin in her hand.

"I suppose she's gone for good," Tess said.

Janice nodded into her palm. "Where does that leave Stuart and Avi?"

"It depends on whether she was an accomplice."

They were still mulling it over when the bell from the front door dinged. LuAnn stood and opened the kitchen door. "Janice! Tess! LuAnn!"

"In the kitchen," LuAnn responded.

The noisy click-clack of heels on the floor and finally saw the woman wearing them. Margaret marched into the kitchen, her eyes bright, her breathing heavier than normal.

"What are you doing here so early?" Tess asked. "Come to get your ill-gotten vanity?"

"No. I wanted to call you last night but thought you might be sleeping."

"Have a seat," LuAnn said, walking to the cabinet for another mug.

"Remember the woman I was telling you about who had the same photograph you brought in, Janice?"

Janice nodded. Not that it mattered much now. It was most certainly Robin.

"I saw that same woman on the news last night." She found a mug and poured herself some coffee, then added milk and sugar.

"You did?"

"With that good-looking anchor, Karl something or other—"

"Mannus?"

She gave a dismissive wave. "I suppose. Anyway, he was interviewing some young man in front of this very inn, and they had a photograph of that very woman in the corner of the screen. Apparently she heads up some archaeological something or other at the university. The boy they interviewed said you found some *bones* in your basement?"

"I guess he went for broke after all," Tess said, her expression one of clear annoyance.

"He must've had a slow news day and used us for another segment after I switched off the TV," Janice reasoned.

The house phone rang just then, and LuAnn went to answer.

"Did you find what you were looking for on the map?" Margaret asked.

"We haven't had much chance to look at it, to be honest."

LuAnn returned to the table, her face stretched into a wide smile. "That was our first call from someone wanting to book a room for the Sternwheel Festival. They saw the inn on the news last night."

"Did you book them?" Tess asked.

"Of course not. I told them we weren't positive the exact date we'd be open for guests, but I took down his name and number and told him we'll call if we can accommodate him."

"Well," Janice said, shaking her head, "I guess Karl might have done us a favor after all."

Michael arrived a couple of hours later with two other strong men. To Janice and LuAnn's consternation, one of them happened to be Robin's neighbor, at the end of her hallway.

"Oh, hey. I've seen you two before. Yeah, you were looking for that Robin chick. You ever find her?"

"Yeah, we did."

Tess glared. "But we lost her again."

He gave her a confused frown, then shrugged. "Well, I'll tell her you're looking for her, if I see her."

The three of them stayed out of the way while the young men filled the moving truck with the beautiful antiques. Janice glanced at the space the Steinway had occupied just the day before. The specialist had come from Columbus and appraised the instrument, letting them know he already had a buyer in mind. When he left, he took the piano with him.

Thorn agreed to relinquish two of his men to help the other three movers load the truck and then unload it at the storage shed.

Isaiah smiled at Janice. "Hey, Mrs. Eastman. You have any idea where Robin is? She didn't show up today. We were supposed to have lunch, but she's not answering texts or calls."

"I don't know where she is." Janice peered closer at him. "Your last name is Wimber?"

He gave her a slow grin. "Um, yes ma'am. Same as always."

"Are you related to the Wimbers across the river?"

"Distantly." He frowned. "Robin asks all kinds of questions about them too. I finally took her to the museum over there so she could see photos of my ancestors."

"Did she find what she was looking for?"

He shrugged. "I told her a story about two of my ancestors who were brothers and how they were killed by a couple of slaves that had escaped. It upset her, but she didn't really explain why."

"You going to help, Isaiah?" Michael called from the sitting room.

Tossing her an apologetic look, Isaiah started to leave, but Janice had a feeling she needed to hear the story of Isaiah's ancestors that had upset a Canadian girl. "Wait. Tell me the story. Michael can take a break for five minutes."

CHAPTER EIGHTEEN

S o, apparently," Janice told Tess and LuAnn when she returned to the kitchen, "according to Isaiah's family history, Rafe and Logan Wimber went after an escaped slave who
had stolen some important family treasure. They pursued him
to this side of the river, and there was a confrontation a couple
of miles from here. Both brothers were shot and killed, apparently by the slave. But he must have gotten away to freedom,
because they never caught him."

Janice had made a side trip to her room upstairs to retrieve
the journal before returning to the kitchen. "Now listen from
a different perspective." She read the part she had read in her
own room earlier.

"So, if the R. and L. Wimbers in this journal are the same
ones Isaiah told me about—and I think it's too coincidental
to believe otherwise—the escape party was accosted by
Rafe Wimber when they got out of the tunnel. But Logan
Wimber wasn't helping Rafe pursue C. He was helping her
escape."

"Family treasure..." LuAnn mulled the words over. "I suppose the baby C gave birth to must have been that treasure."

Janice smiled. "It would seem so. Maybe that's the redeem-
ing part of Rafe's story. That he loved his child."

Tess gave a snort that expressed her opinion without having to say a word. "Keep reading, Janice."

L. Wimber set C. in the wagon and tried to plead with his brother not to take her back to Virginia. To let her have the child and continue on to freedom. When he expressed his desire to marry her, a fit of rage overcame R. and he shot L. point blank in the heart, killing him instantly, then turned his gun on me and said I would never steal another slave away from a master again. I did not know my dear Jason carried his gun, and neither did R. Jason shot him, wounding him. We did not know if he was alive or dead until later when we returned and found his lifeless body lying beside his brother's. C. got to safety, but she was inconsolable about the death of her beloved. My beloved, Jason, is grieved that he was forced to take a life, but he says he would do it again to save mine. I feared the tragedy of the day might have caused me to lose the child I carry. But all seems to be well. Glory to God.

Mr. Siloam rode the ferry with the sheriff to deliver the bodies of R. and L. to the family, just across the river. Mrs. Wimber refused to allow L. to be buried in the family graveyard and insisted they take his body away. Mr. Siloam brought him back to the inn and buried him behind the garden.

When Janice finished reading, they sat in silence for a moment. "Well, that debunks Isaiah's family spin, but it doesn't explain why it upset Robin or why the bones showed up at the inn."

"We can tell you why, ma'am." Robin and Avi stepped into the kitchen. Robin carried a fat folder held together with a large rubber band.

"Look who returned to the scene of the crime," Tess said.

Janice looked at her askance. "Tess..."

"Give them a chance to explain," LuAnn said.

Janice motioned to a couple of chairs. "Sit down, girls."

"First of all," Robin began, "I'm so sorry for not being up-front with the three of you in the first place. But I didn't know you in the beginning. And since I've gotten to know you better this past week, I've just been trying to figure out how to tell you."

Avi nodded as she sat. "She's telling the truth. Neither of us wanted to cause trouble."

"Well, what did you think would come of planting bones in a person's basement, if not trouble?" Tess asked.

"Robin," Janice said, "do you want to start at the beginning?"

"Okay. I told you that I want to write about slaves who made it to freedom by way of the Underground Railroad all the way to Canada and what their lives were like in subsequent years."

"Yes..."

"Well, what I didn't tell you is that one of those slaves, Cecille, was my—our—fifth great-grandmother. She escaped from the Wimber plantation when she was pregnant with our fourth great-grandmother, Willa."

"That's why we were so drawn to this area," Avi added. "We're both fascinated by history. I am through archaeology, and Robin is through books and research."

Janice acknowledged her comment with a nod, then turned back to Robin. "And you met a Wimber right away."

She nodded. "Yes, Isaiah. I was so excited because I thought I could piece even earlier accounts of Cecille's life together through slave records from the Wimber plantation. But their history and our history doesn't even come close to matching. Other than the fact that the brothers died on the same night and there was a slave involved, somehow. It's infuriating that this family denies the love between Logan and Cecille, and denies Rafe Wimber's offenses."

"So, we decided if we could find Logan's bones, we could show the historical society Cecille's written accounts of the night and the love they shared and that would set the record straight."

"So, why leave the bones in the tunnel?" Tess asked.

Robin grinned. "Well, we figured we might get in trouble for digging them up on private property. Plus, I mean, it is sort of grave robbing."

Avi rolled her eyes, and Janice couldn't help but see her unspoken point. She probably dug up bones that weren't even as old as these all the time—just another day on the job. She exhaled and met Janice's gaze. "We know we were being foolish. At first we thought the bones would be on the land that was once owned by Prudence Willard. That's the woman who helped Cecille."

Janice nodded. "We have her journal, which is an account of many of the slaves she helped over several years." She smiled. "Prudence delivered Cecille's baby the night they met."

"I went into the historical society, and a woman allowed me to borrow a few photos of the area. Cecille was at Prudence's home before she was moved to the inn, and she had written a vague description of where the Willards' home was. I had hoped there might be some historical records that could pinpoint it a little better. But I didn't have any luck."

"That is, until"—Robin took the baton—"we remembered in Cecille's writings that she received a letter from Prudence a couple of years after she arrived in Toronto. Prudence told her Mr. Siloam buried Logan behind the garden. It just all clicked."

"But how did you find an unmarked, one-hundred-fifty-year-old grave?"

Avi smiled. "I'm an archaeologist. Finding bones is my day job."

Tess smiled wryly, clearly starting to soften after hearing their honest story. "Bet you didn't dig those bones up during the day."

"Well, no. But we figured with all of the work on the inn and the grounds, it wouldn't be too noticeable." Avi frowned. "But I think I'm the reason you got that ankle. Robin said you stepped in a hole in the yard. We didn't do a good job filling it all back in, in the dark."

That explained that. At least Thorn could stop blaming himself and the crew for being careless.

"I felt so guilty when I saw your ankle," Robin said.

"But I still don't understand why you put the bones in the tunnel," Janice said.

"Well, Robin knew about the tunnel from the workers."

"Humph," LuAnn said. "I had a feeling some of them wouldn't be able to resist doing some exploring."

"We'll have to keep a closer eye on that sort of thing," Tess said. "We don't want to be liable for accidents."

"I'll write it in my notebook."

"We heard you like a good mystery, and the woman at the historical society told me about the journal," Avi continued. "She showed it to me and wouldn't let me touch it, but I assumed you had to have made a copy."

Janice pointed at the pages still on the table. "Who wouldn't have?"

"Exactly," Avi said. "I left the photograph of Cecille and Willa so you'd be curious enough to investigate. And I knew there was a good chance Stuart would call me about the bones."

Janice's defenses rose for her son. "And where does he fit into all of this?"

"Mrs. Eastman, I assure you I started seeing him because I liked him. We've decided very recently we're better as friends than anything more. But we met a few months ago when he was dating a friend of mine. We enjoyed our conversation enough that night that, a few weeks after he stopped seeing my friend, he got my number through the university directory and asked me out."

Disappointment shifted through Janice at the knowledge that there would be no wedding, but she believed Avi.

Tess leaned forward. "Well, you have the bones at the university, and we'll give you the relevant pages of the journal." She looked from Janice to LuAnn for agreement.

LuAnn nodded. "You can tell the story as you see fit."

A few minutes later, after Robin had gone upstairs to eat humble pie for being late and Avi left to return to the university to teach a class, the Inn Crowd poured fresh cups of coffee and discussed everything they'd discovered.

Janice straightened the journal pages.

"You know what I think the most amazing thing in all this was?" Tess said. "That you went upstairs all by yourself this morning to face what could have been a criminal."

Janice sniffed. "I had courage from God—and my hair spray."

LuAnn grinned. "Yes, but it's still a far cry from the woman who was almost too afraid to go to the fourth floor a few weeks ago because of spiders and ghosts."

"Well, no one really believes in ghosts." But Janice realized how far she'd come in facing and overcoming her fears.

"So," Tess said. "Avi's not the one for Stu."

"I guess not," Janice said.

"You know who I think likes him?"

"I was thinking the same thing," LuAnn said. "Robin."

"Me too," Janice said. "They were awfully friendly this morning." She hesitated for a minute. "Think I should mention it to Stuart?"

Janice spent Sunday afternoon dozing and watching an old black-and-white movie alone. Stacy and Larry had gone to the park and the quiet, lazy house had nearly lulled her into an afternoon nap.

Her phone buzzed around five, just when she was dreaming about Lawrence. She fought her way through the veil of her dreamworld and answered, her voice sounding thick in her ears.

"Janice?" LuAnn's voice was a nice surprise. She smiled.

"Hi, Lu."

"Look, something is happening over here at the inn. Can you come right away?"

"Everything okay?" She sat up in the recliner, fully awake now.

"Just come over, will you?"

She made it to the inn in ten minutes flat. If she hadn't taken time to brush her hair and use the bathroom, she might have been there in seven.

When she walked inside, there were at least fifty people milling about the entryway and sitting room. She registered most of the faces present had been members of Lawrence's congregation for many years. "Hi, everyone." She greeted them, although she was thoroughly confused.

"There you are," Tess said. LuAnn tucked her hand through one of Janice's elbows while Tess took her hand on the other side. "Pastor Ben has a surprise for you." She leaned in. "Be nice."

Janice frowned. "I always am."

They walked her into the sitting room and on through to the other end. More confusion set in as she saw, sitting where the Steinway had been a few days ago, another black baby grand piano.

"Oh my word. What is going on?" She looked to her friends, but they suddenly had nothing to say. When Pastor Ben and Paige reached out together and hugged her, she started to get an inkling. "Tess, did we buy this?"

Tess shook her head as Pastor Ben pulled her forward. "We know how much this piano means to you, Mrs. Eastman. So, the board voted unanimously to restore it and present it to you for the inn as a thank-you for so many years serving at the side of a great pastor and man of God."

Speechless, Janice walked forward and ran her fingertips over the sleek black finish. On the back of the piano, there was a plaque.

"Go ahead and read it out loud," LuAnn encouraged.

Her knees felt shaky. "'This piano is donated by the grateful congregation at Christ Fellowship in memory of Pastor Lawrence Eastman'."

Tears filled Janice's eyes. He would be so proud.

She thought of how many ways she'd become stronger lately. More independent. Buying an inn, going into the tunnel alone, confronting an intruder, all the ways she was overcoming fear.

"Will you play something, Mrs. Eastman?" Paige asked.

She sat on the padded bench she had occupied hundreds of times as she accompanied the singing at Christ Fellowship. She put her fingers on the keys, automatically about to start to play Lawrence's favorite hymn. Instead, she adjusted her fingers and began to play another hymn she loved.

'Tis so sweet to trust in Jesus, Just to take him at His word,
Just to rest upon His promise, Just to know thus saith the Lord.

As the people in the room began to sing, Janice looked over the keys and realized that she still had a place. That even though her children were grown and her husband had passed away, she was not without purpose. So much good awaited her, and God had chosen just the right time to start making her brave. She couldn't wait for the next adventure.

Dear Reader,

As I approached the writing of this story, the title *All That Remains,* seemed particularly relevant, not only to the physical plot, which includes scaredy-cat Janice finding a skeleton in her basement, but because with one awful accident on a snowy road, she lost everything that made her who she was for thirty-five years: the love of her life, her ministry position as a pastor's wife, and her home.

I considered the idea: what is left when our identity is suddenly gone? When courage fails? When children leave? When a loved one is snatched away, sometimes cruelly?

Two days before turning in this book, I discovered my answer so beautifully. As a matter of fact, it was Janice who told me. When you are stripped to nothing, all that remains is this: you and *Jesus* in a closet sharing secret pain, passion, and praise. And no matter what life looks like outside of that space, in those moments, when you are on the floor, huddled against a wall, crying out for *something, anything* that brings validation, He gives beauty for ashes, blessing for mourning, hope for despair. He makes you laugh again.

I hope while reading *All That Remains,* you laugh, cry a little, and find hope knowing that God always makes a way in the wilderness when we trust Him with all of our hearts.

Enjoy!

Signed,
Tracey Bateman

About the Author

Tracey Bateman writes from the beautiful Missouri Ozarks where there is much scope for the imagination. With four grown children and two grandchildren, she and her husband are filled with the wonder of God's goodness. They are enjoying empty nesting and watching their growing family live, love, laugh, and thrive.

THE PATH TO FREEDOM

Over forty thousand slaves made their way to freedom in Canada, many of them from Ohio, aided largely by the descendants of the early settlers to the area.

The town of Marietta is small, but what an impact this community had for those without hope, those who could not escape bondage without the help of individuals who were "dedicated to the proposition that all men are created equal." Though the brave slaves and those who ran stations along the Muskingum River are long gone, their legacy lives on both in the pride and kindness of the residents of Marietta, and the grateful descendants of escaped slaves in Canada, who are living proof that each life can and does matter.

Shrimp and Crab Salad

Salad Ingredients:

- 6 oz crabmeat, drained and flaked
- 5 oz small cooked shrimp, chopped
- 1 stalk minced celery
- 1 green bell pepper, seeded and chopped
- 1 onion, diced
- ¾ cup mayo
- 2 tsp finely chopped dill
- 1 tsp Worcestershire sauce
- Salt and black pepper to taste

Salad: Place the crabmeat, shrimp, celery, bell pepper, and onion into a bowl. Stir in the mayonnaise, dill, and Worcestershire sauce until evenly blended. Season to taste with salt and pepper. Refrigerate 1 hour before serving.

Read on for a sneak peek of another exciting book
in the Secrets of Wayfarers Inn series!

GREATER THAN GOLD
by Roseanna White

*Why are we, your creation, so eager to believe the worst of each other,
Lord? So quick to judge what we don't understand? And now all I can
do is cry out, "Father, forgive me!" I know You will. But I fear that poor
girl will forever hate me for the role I've played in all this.*
—Prudence Willard, Marietta Ohio, May 5, 1862

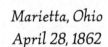

Marietta, Ohio
April 28, 1862

"Pru."

Prudence jumped, splaying a hand over her chest, where
her heart tried with valiant energy to escape its confines.
Her brows knit, even as she chuckled and spun to face her
husband. Dawn was barely a kiss of rose and gold on the
highest tips of the mountains to the east. What would bring

him to the kitchen door of the Wayfarers Inn when he ought to be in their own barn, milking and mucking and feeding?

"Jason. What is it?"

He darted a look over his shoulder, and then over hers, stealing silently across the stone floor until he could lean close to her. "Can thee come home? Only briefly. I have a...gift for thee."

"A gift?" They rarely had money to spare on such things—and though Jason had been known to pick her a bouquet of spring's first flowers, he wouldn't feel the need to come to the inn and tell her of it. Unless...

His smile bore the strain of danger. "A... *package.*"

Try as she might to catch her breath, it wouldn't come. A package—a runaway slave. But why would her contact have brought the poor soul to the farm, to Jason? She pitched her voice to the barest of whispers. "I don't understand."

Her husband leaned closer still, slid a warm hand into its familiar place on her waist, and rested his lips against her ear. Perhaps, if anyone came upon them, they would look like any other couple whose love was as deep as theirs— exchanging a few secret words about nothing but their own affections. "She was alone, my love. Not delivered by any-one. I found her hiding in the haymow. Or, rather, Patience found her."

For a moment, a smile chased away her frown. She could well imagine her pet goose startling the poor creature with a loud honk of greeting. But amusement could not hold out long against the worry. She reached behind her back to untie the apron she'd only tied on ten minutes earlier. "Give me just a moment to find Elizabeth. She will have to get the bread mixed up for me."

Twenty minutes later, Prudence followed Jason into their barn. Morning had crested the mountains while they made their way home from the hotel, and now it spilled golden and sweet through the open barn doors.

Her husband cleared his throat and whistled a three-note tune. Seconds later, a rustling drew Prudence's gaze to the shadows of the back corner stall they used for storing hay. Jason had said nothing on the short drive here about the unexpected visitor he had discovered. But she was always prepared for the worst—people half-starved, their feet bleeding, frostbitten in the winter or suffering heat stroke in the summer.

The young woman who stepped out into the half-shadows, however, was none of those things. She wore a dress the equal of any of Prudence's. Had hair a shade lighter than her own. Skin so pale it barely hinted at any African heritage. And a face so beautiful that a stab of jealousy pierced Prudence before she could even think to guard against it.

Jason touched a hand to the small of Prudence's back. "Sweetheart, this is Tilla."

The adventure had begun. LuAnn Sherrill stood by the stair-case, unable to wipe the grin off her face as Tess checked in their first ever guests at the Wayfarers Inn. People who were even now handing over a credit card to be swiped. People who stood with smiles as they craned their heads back to take in the gorgeous ceilings. People who would go home in a few days and tell their friends what a beautiful place the bed-and-break-fast had been.

They were really doing it. Had *done* it. Against all odds, they'd opened their doors in time for the Sternwheel Festival. Despite all the headaches and false starts, they'd embarked on what was sure to be the greatest adventure of their lives.

"LuAnn!" Adventure sounded an awful lot like panic in the voice of Janice Eastman. The third member of their trio gripped LuAnn's arm and tugged her back into the hallway a few steps, out of sight of the guests. "The elevator's broken."

"What? That can't be. It was just working an hour ago when I took the café's linens down." True, it had been making that strange grinding sound...but that was to be expected in an ele-vator so old it still had gates and had to be hand-operated, right?

Janice gave her a look that LuAnn knew well—one they'd both perfected after years in the public school system. A look that said, *Are you really questioning me?* As if she would make that up.

LuAnn sighed. "Do you think Thorn will know how to fix it?"

"I already called him." Though she didn't exactly look con-fident as she said it. Running her fingers absently through her blonde curls, Janice gazed back down the hall, toward the apparently cantankerous machine. "Though I highly doubt he's ever had cause to work on a hundred-and-fifty-year-old elevator before."

"He's worked on plenty of other things. Surely the skills are transferrable—gears are gears, right?"

"Let's hope so. Go tell Tess, will you, so she doesn't send the guests there? I'll see if I can find someone to help them with their bags on the stairs. Thorn said he'd be here in five."

"Sure." And if Janice failed to round up any younger arms to play bellhop, they'd manage it themselves. Heaven knew they'd all lugged their fair share of loads up those stairs in the last few months. LuAnn slipped around the corner to the front desk, where Tess had smoothed out a brochure about the Sternwheel Festival in front of a man and woman checking in.

While the couple had an on-the-spot debate about which band to see first that evening, LuAnn slid to Tess's side and whispered the latest conundrum into her ear. Not that such news visibly frazzled her after years in the hospitality business. She just gave LuAnn a discreet nod and renewed her smile.

"I bet we can see them both, if we make it a point to keep moving," the young wife on the other side of the desk said. She aimed a bright smile at Tess. "Thanks again for the early check-in."

"It's our pleasure," Tess said with the ease that LuAnn was tempted to practice in a mirror to learn to emulate. Not that she couldn't look calm and collected too, but there was a reason they'd given Tess front-desk duty. "If you're ready, LuAnn will show you up to your room. This weekend we'll keep the front doors unlocked until midnight, but if you happen to return after that, just ring the bell and someone will be down to let you in. Breakfast is served from seven to ten, and if you've had enough festival food at any point and want something a little different, don't forget to check out our soup café."

The couple beamed and reached down for their bags even as one of the servers from the café appeared. LuAnn let out only one small puff of relief and motioned him forward. "Taylor will help with your luggage. You two just follow me." They only had a wheeled, midsize bag and a toiletry bag, so really, they wouldn't even miss the elevator.

Now, that family due to check in at three with a baby and a toddler would be another story altogether. As soon as she had a moment without watching eyes, LuAnn would offer up one mighty prayer that Thorn, their contractor and handyman, could work his skills on the elevator before it became necessary to haul the foldable crib and cot up the staircase.

She led the way toward said staircase, polished to a gleam and looking absolutely beautiful when one had only to haul *oneself* up it. "Have you been here for the Sternwheel Festival before?" She glanced over her shoulder at the couple. They must be the Prescotts—Jackson and Emily. The family with the kids was the Kellys, and the other couples to be checking in were all older.

"Yep, we were here last year and just loved it," Emily said. "The funny thing was that we were walking by this building and Jackson was seeing all the potential and saying what an awesome B&B it would make, weren't you sweetie?"

Jackson ran an appreciative hand up the banister. "Lot of beauty in this old place. I couldn't believe it had sat empty for so long. If we'd had the cash, I would have bought it then and there."

Emily gave an enthusiastic nod that sent her blonde hair bouncing. "When Sasha told us the inn would be open for the festival—well, we couldn't resist. She said her dad had been busy for months, working on it with you guys."

Sasha...her dad. LuAnn turned back to them with wide eyes. "Thorn's daughter! I didn't realize you were friends of hers."

"We all went to college together. We're actually the ones who set up Sasha and Jake."

LuAnn had only met Sasha and Jake Getty once, long enough to exchange smiles and handshakes, but she knew Tory had been thrilled to tears when his estranged daughter decided to move back to Marietta last month. "Well how nice. I bet you guys will have a wonderful visit with them."

At the top of the stairs, LuAnn led the way down the hall. "We put you in Moonlight and Snowflakes. You have a gorgeous view of the river." And a gorgeous view of the room itself when she opened the door for them. The novelty of opening one of those doors and seeing their vision come to life before them definitely hadn't worn off yet.

This room sported a four-poster bed in dark wood that contrasted beautifully with the whites and silvers and blue accents they'd used to decorate it. It was one of her favorites. Of course, so was Woodbine and Roses. And Lilacs and Sage. And, if she was being perfectly honest, all the others.

"Here we are. You two get settled, and if you need anything at all, just let us know."

She stepped out of their way with a smile that felt permanently affixed to her face. Their first guests. Opening day. Dreams coming true.

No broken elevator could possibly ruin this day. Nothing could.

A familiar, masculine voice pulled LuAnn from the kitchen an hour later. It had been a while since she'd seen Bradley Grimes, but she somehow wasn't surprised he'd found time to stop by on opening day. The Realtor had proven himself a friend, and LuAnn palmed one of the wrapped truffles she'd been arranging in a bowl as she headed toward the front to say hello.

"There she is." Janice's eyes twinkled as LuAnn entered the room. "I had a feeling you'd come join us."

LuAnn smiled back and held out the offering of chocolate. "Every guest gets one of these today."

Brad accepted with a grin. "Don't mind if I do. Thanks."

"And look what *he* brought." Janice pointed to a lavish bouquet of flowers on one of the end tables. "Wasn't that sweet?"

Sweet and thoughtful and extravagant—that arrangement had to have cost a hundred dollars, at least. "Well now my truffle looks paltry. Those are gorgeous, Brad. You didn't have to do that."

"I wanted to." His voice was warm. "You ladies deserve it after all the hard work you've put into this place."

"Speaking of which." LuAnn lifted her brows toward her friends. "Did you two need any help? My list is just about completed."

"Nope, I think we're all caught up." Tess slid a finger along the mantel, though there couldn't possibly be as much as a speck of dust on it. Not with the once-over they'd given everything that morning. She turned to study the flowers. "You know what? Those don't belong in here—they belong on the front desk, where everyone can see them the moment they walk in." She charged toward the end table, scooped up the colorful vase, and vanished.

"I had better check on Tory," Janice added, pivoting toward the door.

LuAnn held up a hand. "If he's in the basement, I'll check on him—I was headed down there next anyway. The linens from the café ought to be dry."

Janice didn't argue. "Perfect. I needed to call Stacy back anyway. Thanks again for the flowers, Brad."

He tipped an invisible hat and then leveled his smile on LuAnn. "Mind if I walk down with you? I've been wanting to see how the basement renovations are coming along."

"Of course I don't mind." She led the way, motioning for him to follow. "Not much more than the last time you saw it—but now that the main floor and guest rooms are finished, I imagine we'll focus more down here."

"I'm still amazed at the progress you ladies made in such a short time. I thought you'd be lucky to be open by Christmas."

There'd been plenty of moments when she thought the same, which made her chuckle. "Never underestimate the power of three determined women—or a small town determined to help them." And here they were, open by the second week of September for the town's biggest festival. Sometimes it didn't seem real.

Then the piles of laundry hammered the reality home. She listened as they descended the steps but didn't hear the tumbling of the dryer. Good. She could get those out and folded and delivered back to the soup café before the flood of guests arrived for the three o'clock check-in.

Though, come to think of it, she also didn't hear any tinkering or thumping or humming coming from the elevator shaft—and Thorn was seldom quiet when working. Usually a whistle or hum filled the room around him.

"Hmm." She frowned as she headed through the dim stone chambers, toward where she imagined he'd be working. "Thorn? Are you down here?"

No answer came. She aimed herself toward the elevator doors, knowing her frown was in full-force by now. The gate was open, proving the elevator car was still down here—

probably from when she'd come down with that load of laundry earlier, and then went back up by the stairs for the exercise. And the panel in the wall beside it was open, proving Thorn had accessed the innards somehow or another. But her friend himself was nowhere in sight. "Where could he be?"

Brad stopped beside her. "Maybe he had to check out something on another floor? Or run out to the hardware store?"

Either was a reasonable possibility. Except that a strange glint caught her eye as she angled toward Brad to agree with him. "What's that?"

"What's what?"

"That?" Even as she asked, she was crouching down—careful to keep her specially-chosen opening-day outfit well clear of the not-so-pristine floor—and reaching for what certainly didn't look like an elevator part. Its gleam was far brighter than the age-patinaed brass of the lift, and accented with green as deep as a forest. As deep as...well, as emeralds. "What in the world?"

Her fingers had closed over the links, and she lifted up what was obviously a bracelet. Obviously old. And possibly more expensive than any piece of jewelry she owned, given the lavish diamonds on each side of every emerald. Not to mention the ornate goldwork that cradled all the gems with a flair absent from any of her department-store purchases.

Brad let out a low whistle and crouched down beside her. "Methinks something new was just unearthed yet again at the Wayfarers Inn."

No excitement could fill her veins at the prospect though. Not given the shop rag soaked through with blood that she pointed to next—and the dripping trail of dried red that led toward the exit. Their big adventure had just developed another wrinkle, and it tied her stomach in knots. Because the simple question she'd asked a minute before now felt rather ominous. "Yes but...where's Thorn?"

A NOTE FROM THE EDITORS

We hope you enjoy Secrets of Wayfarers Inn, created by the Books and Inspirational Media Division of Guideposts, a nonprofit organization that touches millions of lives every day through products and services that inspire, encourage, help you grow in your faith, and celebrate God's love in every aspect of your daily life.

Thank you for making a difference with your purchase of this book, which helps fund our many outreach programs to military personnel, prisons, hospitals, nursing homes, and educational institutions. To learn more, visit Guideposts Foundation.org.

We also maintain many useful and uplifting online resources. Visit Guideposts.org to read true stories of hope and inspiration, access OurPrayer network, sign up for free news-letters, download free e-books, join our Facebook community, and follow our stimulating blogs.

To learn about other Guideposts publications, including the best-selling devotional *Daily Guideposts*, go to ShopGuideposts .org, call (800) 932-2145, or write to Guideposts, PO Box 5815, Harlan, Iowa 51593.

Sign up for the Guideposts Fiction Newsletter

and stay up-to-date on the books you love!

You'll get sneak peeks of new releases, recommendations from other Guideposts readers, and special offers just for you . . .

and it's FREE!

Just go to Guideposts.org/Newsletters today to sign up.

Find more inspiring fiction in these best-loved Guideposts series!

Mysteries of Martha's Vineyard

Come to the shores of this quaint and historic island and dig in to a cozy mystery. When a recent widow inherits a lighthouse just off the coast of Massachusetts, she finds exciting adventures, new friends, and renewed hope.

Tearoom Mysteries

Mix one stately Victorian home, a charming lakeside town in Maine, and two adventurous cousins with a passion for tea and hospitality. Add a large scoop of intriguing mystery and sprinkle generously with faith, family, and friends, and you have the recipe for Tearoom Mysteries.

Sugarcreek Amish Mysteries

Be intrigued by the suspense and joyful "aha!" moments in these delightful stories. Each book in the series brings together two women of vastly different backgrounds and traditions, who realize there's much more to the "simple life" than meets the eye.

Mysteries of Silver Peak

Escape to the historic mining town of Silver Peak, Colorado, and discover how one woman's love of antiques helps her solve mysteries buried deep in the town's checkered past.

Patchwork Mysteries

Discover that life's little mysteries often have a common thread in a series where every novel contains an intriguing whodunit centered around a quilt located in a beautiful New England town.

To learn more about these books, visit Guideposts.org/Shop